WORLDS LIKE DUST

Part 1

Lazlo Ferran

Worlds Like Dust

Part 1

Lazlo Ferran

PRINTING HISTORY
First Edition

Printed in 12 point Times New Roman

Published by Future City Publishing, London.

Front Cover by Ashley Buttle and Lazlo Ferran.

Acknowledgments

Thanks to Ash, Derek, Pedro and David.

Contents

Prologue

It's been over ten years since Gary Enquine sent my friend Przeltski to a certain death. Not one day has gone by without the memories of that battle prowling my mind like a waking nightmare. Many times, I have woken in a cold-sweat thinking about it. I will not rest, cannot rest, until Gary Enquine has been brought to justice and been forced to pay for his cowardice. Ten years; it's a long time but I can be patient. Personal journal entry of Jake Nanden for 2101, Feb 3. 1.

In Unknown Place, Unknown Universe, Stone warned his father, Jake, that the Ischians were planning to invade Earth … .

***

Chapter One

10 weeks until Zero Hour

"Work!" the Ischian guard's voice blared.

The tall slave, digging in the Minnesota iron mine open pit, suddenly straightened up and yelled, "I've had e-fuckin-*nough*!" through gritted teeth.

"The sun's finally drilled into his brain!" whispered the man two places down the chain.

The alien barked, "Work!" through his helmet translator twice more.

The second time, he pointed the ubiquitous clover leaf laser rifle at the slave.

Driving his shovel into the spill heap, the tall man glared at the ten foot alien:

"Water! I need water and I ain't gonna dig no more until I *git* some! See this?"

The slave wiped a slick of water from his forehead and let it drip from his palm. He added:

"Called sweat! More than a cup full on my face right now! We get two cups per day! We're *all* gonna die if you don't treat us better. Then I bet you're gonna have your ass kicked by your boss for letting your … precious … *slaves die!"*

The man's voice rose towards an enraged howl with every word:

"Ischian bastards! I won't do no … more … shit … for … you!"

The Ischian stared through his UV visor at the strange, hairless and white, human slave. This one wasn't going to be any use. He aimed the rifle at the slaves head and pulled the trigger slowly back with his claw. Immediately, a high pitched whine could be heard. An instant later, he fired.

The first second burst cut a neat hole straight through the man's head, with the beam exiting his face and cutting into the soil at his feet. Before he could fall, the Ischian soldier waved the gun barrel to slice off the man's head and brought the barrel back to slice the man neatly in half at the waist. Curiously, the head hit the ground an instant before the torso and legs crumpled either side of it. Partly cauterised, the body parts smoked and steamed between gouts of blood which began to form rivulets between the chunks of dug soil.

The men either side both tried to pull away but the anchor chain held them to the dead man's legs. One of them vomited.

"Back to work!" the Ischian's translator bellowed. "I'll get the gang-master to cut you two loose!"

The slave to his right whispered to the man, bound to the corpse leg, "What was his name?"

"I dunno. Brown, I think. Something like that."

"Brown! Brown!" the first man began to chant.

Soon all the men in the mine had thrown down their picks and shovels and chanted, "Brown! Brown!"

One hundred slaves were taken out that night and buried alive.

***

9 weeks until Zero Hour

"*Hey*! *Monk*! Watch where you're *going*! I didn't fight a *war* just to … ."

The drunk had barged into me on a sidewalk, under the vast Trion Corporation Building in Washington DC. It caught me by surprise. I had just been trying to grieve for my lost – my murdered – son, Stone, but the feelings wouldn't come; perhaps because I hadn't *seen* his death. Now everything seemed out of place, like a broken tooth. I had already been trying to cope with the grief of losing my wife, Katie, and my younger son, Daniel, to the Ischian invaders.

By chance, I had downloaded the last com message from Katie, just before I left my apartment on the Moon, that day; the day the aliens entered our Solar System. So while in transit, I had played it back. At first, I thought I watched actors in a movie; Daniel's crushed body on the lap of Katie. She leaned at an odd angle against a wall, with a strange, red stain on the chest of her suit. She must have taken her headband off and placed it on something to record herself.

"Darling," she said. "Daniel's dead! I am dying. J5's been attacked! There's not much time! I didn't … ." She gasped for her last breaths. I shudder each time I play this back in my mind. She continued, "They didn't even have time to call me back into the Service! It's a mess! You *have* to survive and fight them! You were right, Stone was right and I was *wrong*! Those fuckin' aliens are *here*! But I just wanted to say I love you, very, very *much*! The other day…" She smiled. "… Daniel said he loved you. I had to tease him to get him to say it." Her eyes seemed to cloud over, as if she were looking as far away as heaven. "But you know what teenagers are l- … ." Her voice ended and the rest of the transmission, two minutes of it, showed a view of their two bodies, lying inert. Explosions jogged the picture occasionally and distorted the sound. Then it went blank. And now, so did I.

Into the void came a memory:

My first encounter with an alien terrified me. The beast, almost black in colour, had very long arms and hands like spades. It had a head like a jackal with very long ears. It seemed to be constantly moving, as if struggling to hold its position in the thick air, which made it seem even more like an apparition. Men fell back before it, either out of fear or awe.

The admission that she had been wrong, and Katies' brave smile, made me love and ache for my wife even more. Now Earth belonged to the Ischians and the three people I loved the most were gone; wiped out!

Those images flashed through my mind again, even as the man shouted at me on the street.

Nothing fits!

So the man's shouting wasn't unusual, but I stopped. Something about his voice sounded familiar. I turned.

"What you *looking* at?" he spat.

I couldn't see his face in the shadows but his dark hair had been pulled back into a pony-tail. Neon light reflected off his vodka bottle as he swung it menacingly. The hot, sticky rain dripped into my eyes under the alien, bell jar dome. It was late and I wanted to go home. I nearly turned back and walked on:

"Do I *know* you?" I replied.

"I seriously *doubt* it mister. Or should I call you Reverend? Heh! Heh!"

I retraced my steps and peered closely at the bellicose face under the peak of his army-surplus cap.

"DeTunne! What the hell … ! Good to see you!"

I reached out to slap him playfully on the back but he knocked my arm away. Quick as lightning, he drew an X.10 laser pistol from somewhere and pointed it at my head.

"Well, well, *well*! *General* Jake Nanden. *Mr* … now! Funny how fate conspires against us sometimes, isn't it?" He took a long pull from the neck of the bottle, almost draining the last of its spirit, and threw it against a wall. "I always said if this day ever came… if I were ever *this* lucky, I would *kill* you. And now I have you in my sight." He waved the weapon carelessly from side to side and his eyes closed for a moment. I weighed the chances of knocking it from his hand and diffusing the situation.

Not good!

DeTunne had been one of my best grunts. Because he had been career soldier, it surprised me to see him here. I knew his reactions would still be faster that most and he had a cat's instinct for survival.

The X.10 was an obsolete hand weapon. An early Trion laser, heavy on juice and underpowered, most people would fit it with a spreader to inflict messier wounds but it could still kill instantly at short range. This range would be classed as very short.

"Why?" I replied. "I don't understand. The last I heard, you were doing well; a Major, wasn't it?"

"Ha! Yeah. Before I was kicked out. 'Superannuated,' I think the term used to be. Didn't you *know*? After your trial, and subsequent *conversion* to *full human*, for *all* to see, the lot for us mere replicants got even *worse*! *If* that's possible! Shall I tell you what I do now, to make a living?"

I swallowed. "What?"

"I'm a blanker! *First Class,* mind. Oh yeah, there's a *market* for former military men down here in ol' DC. Didn't you *know*? I guess there are perverts for *every* possibility!"

I couldn't imagine DeTunne letting somebody take over his body remotely, which is what a blanker does, but I could see he wasn't lying.

"Why don't we … ."

"Don't *interrupt* me, Nanden. At least you can let me have *my* say. That's better!" His slurring had become worse. "I could kill you now but you know what? I actually think you're *still* an outcast! Even *now*. Yeah. A monk! Ha! Jake Nanden. Who would have thought you'd become a monk! I can hardly *believe* it! *Go now*! Before I change my mind! But if we ever meet *again*...!"

He fired the laser to my right, making a ragged crater in the building's concrete and showering us both in grit. While *I* ducked, he just laughed. I backed away a few paces and then turned.

"Oh … one other thing!" he added.

I stopped again.

"That girlfriend of yours, Jena. Guess who she was with after Lincoln?"

I shook my head slowly.

"*Me*! Yeah! She left old Lincoln for me! Ha! Well, actually she didn't have much choice, so she might not be happy, like, but … ."

He rambled on but the shot had hit home. I walked on, quickly. I heard his voice again:

"Mind you, I hear Lincoln's dead now too … . Ha! Ha! Losing your ex and your son, all in one lousy year! Must really *suck*!"

My legs almost went from under me.

The invasion of Earth by the Ischians had not shocked me like almost everyone else. Stone had warned me and I had time to make some preparations, but the invasion had been breathtakingly swift. Within days, I found myself completely cut off, under this great dome, from those I loved; my mother, my wife, Katie, my second son and now my oldest son.

But everyone had been in the same boat; everyone had either lost someone close or believed they had. Here, in the stifling Ischian bell-jar, no news came in and none went out. And even beyond this, no news left Earth and none arrived. The aliens blocked all traffic; radio, powered transport and even laser.

I knew it likely that my son, Stone, had been killed but I had no proof. Yet! But DeTunne's shot echoed the doubts that whispered incessantly in my mind. DeTunne's parting words reverberated like cannon-shells exploding in my head. They were followed by an insistent little voice. "Stone is dead! Stone is dead!"

I tried to ignore DeTunne and focused on putting one foot in front of the other until I finally turned the corner and breathed out.

***

9 weeks until Zero Hour

Hani Deitner peered through the gap between the two fallen structural beams on USAC Station 5. He could see a lot of dust and rubble beyond. Sparks jabbed from the end of one swinging cable, each time it periodically touched a fallen metal cross-member. At his feet, lay the body of a dead Ischian. It had been almost bisected at the waist. Its orange blood had oozed onto some debris and solidified.

'Dead at least a few hours, I reckon,' he thought. 'Lucky grunt who got it!'

Hani stooped to look at the mess oozing out of the body more closely. A messy pile of flesh, like giant pink spaghetti, lay outside the severed hips.

'Intestines … just like us.'

Something small crawled on the flesh.

'A fly! I thought we eliminated those, off Earth!'

He could also see something like a kidney but at that moment the rancid smell of decaying Ischian flesh hit his nostrils. He stood up like a fired bolt:

'Ugh! Jesus. This is a mess. Don't look safe around here to me! Why the hell didn't Sarge just leave me as a Corporal? I never wanted responsibility anyway!'

He peered more closely at the fallen beams and swinging electrical cable.

'Looks like there just might be a way through…'

Seargeant Deitner picked up the alien's black laser rifle, complete with the ubiquitous green 'clover leaf' label. It was still cocked. The charge showed half full.

'May as well use it … . Better than this shit!'

He thought about dropping his own rifle but he had never used an alien laser before, only seen it being used. Putting his own X.259 into its shoulder holster, he gingerly slid his leg through a gap and ducked his head under a beam. He could just about reach down far enough to place his boot squarely on a mound of rubble. Transferring his weight from left to right foot, he used his free arm to pull himself through.

His sucked his breath in at a violent jolt, followed by the deafening percussion. He felt the beam in his hand rocking from side to side.

'Please God, don't let anything fall on me.'

He closed his eyes and waited a few seconds for the shaking to stop. He recalled the first alien he had encountered. Dressed in formidable white armour and standing nearly ten feet tall, it had strode towards him and aimed is laser straight at his head. Through its visor, he could just make out a terrible canine grin when it had been about to fire. Only a lucky shot from one of the other grunts had saved him. He shuddered every time he remembered it.

"Fuckin' alien dog shite! Why did they have to pick on us! There must be a million species out there; whole planets with amoebas as the apex predator or even three-legged kangaroos! But no, they had to pick us! It's just shit, that's all… Just bloody shit! If I ever…"

His rambling thoughts were interrupted by another explosion and more debris hitting his face. He spotted a slight movement down a corridor to his right. Before he even looked up, he had raised the barrel of the laser rifle. Only instincts saved him.

A beam of blinding white light tore across his vision. He felt something searing his trigger hand but he had no time to look down. The instant his barrel pointed at the moving shape, he fired. Another piercing white line shot out from the barrel to the shadow which had now become an Ischian grunt. Hani's shot would be the luckier. The alien stared at the neat hole in the left side of its chest but Hani had already began to swing the laser barrel. The white beam of light sliced the dark air and the alien at an oblique angle.

Deitner released the trigger when he saw another movement. Behind the first Ischian stood another, stooping to pick up his laser.

Yanking the laser back down, Hani fired a short burst into the backside of the second alien. He held the trigger back for a long burst. The alien exploded into a smouldering ball of flesh, bone, orange blood and flapping suit material. The first alien had been so nearly severed in two that the top half of his body simply peeled away from the bottom half and fell to Hani's right. It landed with a squelching sound, an instant after the second exploded.

"Wow! These are good!" Hani stared at the end of the Ischian laser. His elation would be short-lived. "But we don't stand a chance if they all have these!"

He crept carefully towards to the two dead aliens, eager to know what they had been doing.

Only the head and arms remained of the second alien. They were on top of something; something pale and human-coloured. Hani dragged the remains of the alien away.

"Bastards!" he exclaimed, under his breath.

A dead female USAC grunt lay naked in front of him. Her clothes were ripped off and, apart from a neat laser hole through her heart, her wounds were claw marks, down her chest. Hani looked at the first dead alien. It wasn't wearing gloves.

"Now I know what you were doing..! Fuckers!" He emptied a short laser burst into the alien's groin. "Now, if you even get to the alien Heaven, you won't have anything to fuck with!"

'Now I feel much better' he thought.

He finally remembered to look at his trigger hand. The duratex glove material had cut away on the outside of his thumb. He saw some blood when he examined the rent but it didn't look serious.

"Fuck!"

Deitner kept the clover leaf laser in a firing position and set his jaw before moving off at a lope down the wreckage-strewn corridor, towards the main Operations Room of Station 5.

'If Colonel Dalgleish is still alive, that's where she'll be!'

His orders from the Staff Sergeant had been to find the Colonel, relay the squad status and return with orders, if there were any. It had been nearly six hours since any contact with any other squads or the chain of command. He left only the dead Sergeant and two grunts behind.

'Why the hell there is any air left in here, I will never know!' he thought. 'Tribute to the tough design of these old stations, I guess! Is that a light?'

At last, in the eerie shadow-play of a corridor filled with dust and lit only by shorting wires, Deitner saw a glint of hope. There seemed to be a faint light, somewhere ahead.

"Maybe somebody else is alive!" he thought.

He reached a hatch, half torn off its hinges. The faint light leaked out from behind it. He coughed, as some dust went straight down his throat, and peered around the edge of the hatch.

"Anybody here?" he whispered. "Anybody *here*?" he shouted, putting aside his fear of another alien encounter.

"Hey! Who's there!" somebody answered.

"Hey! I'm … ." Deitner's words were cut off as yet another explosion threw him to the ground. It winded him for a moment but he crawled to the hatch, dragging his weapon.

Several arms heaved the hatch open and pulled him through. Two Sergeants propped him against the wall and pulled off his helmet. One of the Sergeants, blonde with glasses, fetched a steel mug of water and offered it to him

"Thanks! Is Colonel Dalgleish here?"

"She sure is, soldier. You've reached the last outpost of sanity in the whole Jupiter system!"

***

9 weeks until Zero Hour

As she looked out over Earth, A-schian'bakî's inner eye filled the memories of her beautiful Lu-kshîa's launch day. It played back so clearly in her mind that she could easily convince herself, for a just a few precious moments, that they were still in Prima1, just over one year ago:

"Reverse all reactor thrust." A-schian'bakî stared straight ahead, out of the main bridge viewing ports of the Lu-kshîa. The lights of Primal space port sparkled in the night sky over Ito's northern hemisphere, itself lightly dusted by the lights of unsleeping cities. Their citizens would not be aware that the greatest battleship the Ischian Imperial Fleet had ever built would soon leave its dock for the first time. Top secret ships always had nighttime debuts.

The tall, dark-furred Ischian flexed her claws inside her footware and leaned forward slightly so that the sudden rearward jolt of the ship hardly moved a whisker on her face. The hull of the vast ship seemed to groan as her command turned into the unimaginable power of the battleship's drive.

'This is power! This is living!' she gloated to herself.

She mused that the ship and its namesake, the Leader of the High council, did share some physical similarities, especially with the latter in a supine position. She chuckled at her joke.

'Two thousand four hundred arms long. Four hundred and eighty wide. Nearly nine arms longer than the Royal K'ynnuia; the previous record holder!'

The identifying 'K' on the vast flank of the ship had been her idea. It had not been the next letter available but she had lobbied hard to get it because 'K' had been the ancient pictoglyph for 'Purity,' but also the first letter of the Royal K'ynnuia. Now she would prove that she really did have the military blood in her veins which her family so cherished.

"Are we clear of the dock?" she asked her Second in Command. He walked to the side viewing port and watched the dock end slide silently past the flank of the ship. Always economical with words, his only virtue in her mind, he waited until he could reply:

"Clear!"

The slight purpling of space around the battleship, caused by the effect of the engines on the gravitational field as the ship moved, pleased her.

"Let's find out where we are going, then." She turned, and led her 2IC to a cream coloured cabinet at the back of the bridge. Taking keys from the chains around their wrists, they both inserted them in the double lock and turned their keys together at her nod. She withdrew the small canister, removed the tablet from it and replaced the canister in the cabinet. Her 2IC closed the cabinet, which locked automatically.

A-schian'bakî returned to her position near the front viewing port. The tablet could be read, felt or listened to but she chose to read it, to herself:

> You will take the Imperial Battleship Lu-kshîa
> through the first M-class Transfer Port and
> then use nuon to reach the Colonists on Bek-
> su. There, you will make contact with the Im-
> perial agents and reinforce them, in prepara-
> tion for Peaceful World. Once they have supe-
> riority, you will use the beta channel to its
> usual destination and await instructions there.

A-schian'bakî smiled and suppressed a chuckle. 'First M-class Transfer Port' was military-speak for the first wormhole created by the Colonists. 'Nuon' she knew as the codename for the G8D, itself a curious acronym for the secret drive, first tried on Lu-kshîa and copied from – the Colonists. The 'beta channel' was informal military parlance for the wormhole to the human's planet in the past, created by – the Colonists. The term 'Peaceful World' amused her most of all. The humans certainly wouldn't laugh at all if they knew the irony of this code name.

'This is going to be an interesting mission!' she thought.

Too bad things had gone so terribly wrong since then.

***

9 weeks until Zero Hour

Back at my apartment, I made myself a coffee and changed into dry clothes. I tried to dry the condensation, which constantly falls inside the dome and which people laughably called 'rain,' from my hair. Within minutes, it had become soaked again. I showered and rubbed the mirror so I could look at my reflection; an old face with receding white hair. I wondered how I would look with a pony-tail. I pulled the cord on the air-con unit but nothing happened.

Nothing works!

I felt tempted to kick the broken air-con unit but my vows forbade it.

I switched to the news channel on the com. It seemed to consist of nothing but pictures of the gigantic alien space ship now poised over the North Pole; cruisers, like tiny dots, around it to emphasise its size. The picture had been authorised for broadcast, just to intimidate us further.

"All Rebel air transportation has now ceased in the northern hemisphere!" the pal faced newsreader said. "All unauthorised vehicles can now be destroyed instantly! Another Imperial ship like this will be arriving soon and take up station at the South Pole."

I switched the com off. I wondered if the newsreader had a laser pointed at his head while he read. And what did 'soon' mean? Most people were in a state of communal depression at the dome's impregnability and the dominance of the huge ships. My military training didn't allow me to feel this. I just knew that time was running out.

An image of Katie came into my head again; of her holographic image jamming with me long ago:

She had been playing one of her songs, I had been trying to persuade my faulty nano-generator or n-gen to construct a flute from the plans she had transmitted. We laughed so much. I chuckled at the memory. For a moment, I felt again the joy.

My mind ran over the same set of thoughts for the thousandth time:

I was one of the few who knew the invasion was imminent and yet still I could do nothing, still I seemed to have lost all those I love!

Only one other thing broke my almost constant depression; the conversation with DeTunne. It wasn't just the threat of the laser; such things were common in DC these days. Even I, wearing a habit, got mugged regularly; usually for nothing. No, many other aspects of the conversation bothered me. What he said about Jena, hurt the most. Could it be true? Had she really been sleeping with De-Tunne? I felt a sharp pain in the pit of my stomach, each time I thought about the possibility of her sleeping with DeTunne. It shocked me. Did this mean my grieving for Katie and Daniel could be coming to an end? Did I still have feelings for Jena? DeTunne could only have sought her out to spite me but then she either felt she had to spite me or felt vulnerable. The latter hurt more because I had never found any vulnerability in her, myself. Did that make me naïve or simply stupid?

I paced up and down for a while, trying to stop the vicious slew of thoughts raging through my head. Unable to do so, I swung open the glass door to my veranda, just about the only luxury available on the open market. I went outside and sat on the old red plastic chair, which a previous tenant had left. Through the dome, far above, one could still see clouds, on the very rare occasions when it became very hot outside, so reducing the condensation effect inside. Occasionally, I would still see a bird, or even an alien cruiser, passing on that peculiar diffraction-curve path. It calmed me. Any connection with the outside world calmed me.

Why would she do it? Had her sense of self-worth dropped so low since things went bad on the Moon?

It came as a shock to my system. And that, to a grieving man, came as a surprise in itself. I sat down and put my head in my hands.

And I thought things couldn't get any worse! Stuck on Earth by a freak coincidence, no word from outside, not even from Katie or Stone, and trapped in a furnace, controlled by ten feet tall aliens! And now this! Now I am getting angry!

***

I slept even less than usual that night. Fortunately, I had a meeting in the morning to occupy my mind. We all tried to carry on living as if things were normal, it's the human way in times of crisis, but very few of us had much meaning to our lives any more. Nobody could leave DC so only those with work in the local service industries, particularly utilities or the Health Service, really had much to do. Local news agencies were the exception to this. For some reason, the Ischians allowed them to continue operating and everybody felt hungry for any news they could get, even gossip.

Among this background noise, of course there had to be resistance. Many secret networks had sprung up and I would meet clandestinely that day with my contact, in a coffee bar near Capitol Hill.

"Any news?" I asked Don, handing him an insipid coffee and wiping the sweat off my forehead with the back of my hand. Don was first-cousin of Adam, son of my friend and Governor of California, Gary Enquine.

"Not much to tell. Still nothing from outside. Nothing seems to get through. There are rumours that some USAC forces are still resisting… somewhere out there. Nobody knows where. Maybe Mars. Some say Jupiter. My money's on the latter."

I watched the top of his bald head bob up and down like a shiny pink float in the sea, as he formulated his news and spooned his coffee, thoughtfully.

A waiter passed. I switched subjects quickly.

"I hear the Ischians have passed a new directive. Directive forty-nine: 'No Humans to drive sky-cars without direct permission from the Overseer.'"

"Yes, that will play havoc with the smugglers! Ha! It's okay. He's gone now."

"Is there any way to bribe any of these slave-masters? Some of them look... corruptible," I asked.

"That's hardly usual talk for a man of the cloth, is it?" he answered, grinning.

Only a year before the Ischian invasion, work been completed to raise the Capitol Building onto an island, two hundred feet above its surroundings. This would allow the construction of two, ten-lane underpasses for the massively increased sky-car traffic that accompanied the resettling of Earth. I glanced up through the window at the noble, white building high above me and shook my head sadly. Few souls were brave enough to enter the building now, infested as it had become with Ischian slave-masters, who were in turn ruled over by the Ischians.

Something niggled in the back of my mind. I found it particularly hard to focus.

Only when I went to the counter to order our last round of coffee, did the niggle make itself clear. A light came on in my head. I tried to control my sudden excitement. I had become wary of anything that seemed hopeful.

We had never visited the same cafe twice consecutively but even when we ran out of cafes and had to re-visit one, we always sat at a different table. I made sure the coffee grinder nearby belted out enough decibels before telling Don what had occurred to me:

"Don, something happened to me last night. Something about it has been bothering me all night. Now I think I know why."

"What happened?"

"Well, I ran into this guy who served under me on Io, years ago, more than twenty in fact. DeTunne, his name is. Anyway, to cut a long story short, he told me that he had been seeing one of my ex's before the invasion."

"So?"

"Well, never mind that but he also said that *her* ex, a guy called Lincoln, recently *died* … ."

"And?"

"The day I arrived at DC Port, I called her … you know, to catch up…"

"Yeah...?"

"She said she was fine. I asked if she was still seeing Lincoln and she said; yes!"

"So what?"

"That was the day before the dome went up! If DeTunne knows Lincoln is dead, then maybe there *is* a way for news to get in… She never *mentioned* that anything had happened to him! Don't you see; he was okay on the day I arrived!"

"It's not much to go on … . Are you sure of your facts?"

"Yeah! We gotta find this guy. He's dangerous but maybe he knows something. Maybe he *can* get news."

I didn't mention that DeTunne thought Stone to be dead. I didn't want to think about it.

***

9 weeks until Zero Hour

An-Hnadhîa leaned against the warm hull of his beloved J-Class Crawler; J-Crawler for short. Sol had begun to dip below the red dune to the west, marking the end of another Earth day and the beginning of the cold night. He had just enough time for one last pipe of chum before joining his crew in the mess. He spat out the gum, which fizzed with the vital Nitrogen needed to sustain his lungs in the thin atmosphere. He quickly drew down the hot, spicy narcotic; too much and he would pass out – hence the pipe – too long and he would die. But he couldn't resist it. This was the only moment a commander of his rank could have some solitude and, even then, only by ordering his men to stay inside. He could only see one of the three sentries, who nodded once before An-Hnadhîa looked away.

Ironically he had paid ten i-tan for the chum, a huge amount, but the going rate on the Ischian black-market while, only a few miles away, Earth tribesmen were buying it for one-hundredth of this amount.

'Damned politics!' he thought. 'I wish I could drive straight in and take it now!'

He let the narcotic envelop his thoughts so that all anger became like a distant speck of red light. He laughed at it and felt himself floating on a sea of green peace and tranquillity. His alarm suddenly blared to remind him to switch back to Nitrogen gum.

"Damn!"

Within minutes of entering the J-Crawler's mess, An-Hnadhîa had toasted his squad and they launched into their fibrofil meal; this time roasted k'ynnuia and katahh washed down with a crude jzu-serinî. Yes, his squad always ate well. He saw to that. If he closed his eyes so that he couldn't see the green concentrate formed into various shaped and textures, he could convince himself he sat in an at least average restaurant on Ito, home planet of the Ischians now that Isch-su had been ruined.

A sudden commotion, to his right, drew the Commander's eyes. One of the non-rank soldier jumped up and pointed a Dn-57 across the mess to one of the other grunts. The long-barrel laser had not yet been deployed as standard issue and, for just an instant, An-Hnadhîa wondered how it had come to be there. Then a thin jet of something transparent arched across the mess from its barrel and hit the other grunt on the muzzle. The sudden silence of the room became then filled with howls of laughter.

"Water!" he exclaimed.

Although plants taken from Ich-su to Ito actually produced water as a by-product of their 'osmosis,' all plant-life on Ito grew inside protective shields and barely enough water could be produced to provide for the population's needs. But water seemed relatively common here that one of the grunts had thought to bring a toddler's toy water-gun model of the laser to Earth. An-Hnadhîa slapped his thighs and clapped his paws in delight.

This one will make history! Water used for fun. A 'water-fight'!

***

9 weeks until Zero Hour

As soon as he felt able to stand, Seargeant Hani Deitner presented himself to Lieutenant Colonel Dalgleish. She swung to face him from the communications control panel at the prompt of an immaculately barbered Major. Deitner felt jealous.

"Sergeant … ?"

"Deitner, Colonel. Reporting from Station B Company, Baker Company *sir*!" He snapped his heels as best he could but the Colonel stared straight into his eyes.

"How long have you been a Sergeant?"

"Let's see. About eighteen hours sir!"

"Hm. And your Company? B Company … a training company … before all *this*."

"Yes sir!"

"Alright Sergeant. No need to be quite so … formal. We'll soon all be dead anyway. I'm amazed you *are* still alive. How many of you are there and where?"

"Just two grunts sir. The Squad Sergeant died. His last action was to promote *me* to Sergeant … "

She smiled and her blue eyes reminded him of something. He couldn't quite place it.

"Where?"

"Near the hanger deck Colonel. On one of the defence gantries … but … well, there ain't much of it left. Only two sealed compartments left and we were firing out in the open. The others will be out of air now and back inside."

"Did you see any other squads out there?"

He shook his head, thinking. "There was some firing a hundred yards to our left, over an hour before I left. Looked like two, maybe three shooters but it stopped. Can't say for sure but I think we were the last on that side of the Station."

"Enemy strength?"

"Well sir. Seems unlimited! I would say five, maybe more, cruisers, fully manned. No damage that I could see. Our lasers barely touch *them*! Any case, they stay well out of range... unless they're trying to draw our fire, like they do, you know?" He didn't mean to let despair creep into his voice but she heard it.

"Alright. I know it's bad. But it's not over yet. I have an idea." She swung away from him, said something to one of the Coms Officers sitting in a high-backed seat to her left and stood up:

"Okay. Gather round. I have come to a decision!"

The noise of battle continued, with explosions rocking the large control room every few seconds, but all eyes were fixed on the Colonel. She seemed to be the only point of calm in the tornado of battle.

"Corporal Deitner, here, has just arrived from our starboard side. As we suspected, we have almost no defences left intact. Perhaps a hundred of our own out there, if that. We can no longer defend Station 5."

There were murmurs and groans at this.

"But as you *also* know, we cannot surrender," she continued. "We know, from past experience … that the

Anu … Ischians, do not take prisoners. At least, not in this war. And I am not prepared to sacrifice any more troops on a Station that is doomed. Five days ago, we managed to get our last message through to S.4, Mars, and they confirmed they still had three operational cruisers. Before they were cut off, they confirmed they were dispatching one to S.5. That cruiser, if it's still operation, should now be less than two days from us. I believe we should try to rendezvous with that ship and head for Mars where the only concentration of USAC forces in the Solar System seems to be left. At least there, we can do some good!"

There were nods from around her audience. She cleared her throat:

"The question is … how? We have no cruisers left of our own. Its true S.5 has its own motors but these are all down now. They are all beyond repair. We have no means of transiting."

Fists hit desks and palms. Her men were frustrated and angry. She started to pace up and down:

"We have just one card left to play!"

Men looked at each other, confused, but intrigued. She stared at her feet for a moment.

"It's a crazy idea, but, it's our only hope. And not much one at that!"

Her troops loved that.

"Who remembers the old hangar deck?" she asked.

"The old museum?" somebody asked.

"Yes. The museum. Its hatch is sealed off now; welded closed years ago. If any of you visited before... all this, you will remember an old Mark 7 MCS."

"That old thing? The one that Nanden took to Ganymede?"

"That's the one."

Astonished faces broke into smiles of polite disbelief.

"Let me finish. It can still be made to *work*. There are so few of us left now that we can all fit on board. Its reactors … I know because my first duty as Colonel was to sign off its Ten Year Service – yes, it's still listed as Operational – are still functioning properly."

Her audience hung on her every word.

"My plan is that we break open the hanger doors, eject everything in that hanger as a distraction, hope that we are not noticed and make our escape." There were muted claps.

"Oh and while we're at it, leave a little surprise on board S.6 for the Space Dogs!"

Now there came a roar of approval and wolf-whistles.

"We may not get very far, but we will
go … down … fighting!"

With that, Colonel Diana Dalgleish raised her fist and grinned, showing the the kind of heroism USAC grunts liked. "Deitner!" she barked. "I want you to choose four men and get ready to leave with them. You are going to round up every man you can find alive and tell them that, in six hours from now, at twenty-two hundred, they must be in the old hanger or get left behind. You two," she said pointing at two Sergeants, unshaved and stripped to their vests and shorts at the back of the room, "Pfenigshaven and Richardson. You are our best two Strategic Planning brains. The aliens have weapons we don't have. The only way we can win this war is to get our hands on those weapons and use them against the sonsofbitches. You two are relieved of all other duties until you come up with a plan to take one of their cruisers. Is that clear?"

Both grunts stood to attention, grinned and shouted, "Yes! Sir!"

"Now, everybody else, I will see you in fifteen minutes in the planning room. We have lot of work to do and we have to do it all in six hours."

She came over to Deitner and leaned close to him. "I have been planning this since yesterday. When you find any men alive, try to space them in small groups evenly around the Station. Every third group is to retreat one half of the way to the Hanger every hour. Some must keep to the top of the station, some to the bottom. With any luck, the enemy will not realise what we're up to. Now get your men and go. Take all the Oxygen and ammunition you can carry. And take one of those trucks as far as you can. Take the east connector; it's fairly clear. Good luck Lieutenant!"

"But … ?"

"I promoted you."

"But I only just got promoted to Sergeant!"

"You have combat experience, plenty of it, you have a clover leaf and you know how to use it."

***

9 weeks until Zero Hour

A-schian'bakî snapped out of her reverie and grimaced, which made her jowls quiver. It was an uncouth habit she had tried to curb since her youth, unsuccessfully. She looked down again at the white pole of the pretty blue planet below.

"Any word from the Bak-schi, yet?" she asked her 2IC.

"Not yet Commander."

After decelerating out of hyper-space near the human planet, the crew had only seen Ear^h rotate twice before the Lu-kshîa reached her planned station in her orbit. That was nearly half an Earth-year ago, or one hundred and fifty rotations of the blue planet. The planet spun, almost imperceptibly slowly compared with Ito, marking out time.

The Bak-schi, Lu-kshîa's sister ship and second of the type to be completed, would arrive and take up its position over the opposite pole, within another sixty revolutions of the pretty little blue planet.

A-schian'bakî turned to her 2IC:

"When the Bak-schi is here, the first of the Bekian Commando Units will descend to the planet's surface and spread out to enslave the remaining free humans. Escape, for them, is still possible but not for long! Already, one of my crack units of Ischian Imperial Guards has spent almost a month on cold, iron-rich Earth. An-Hnadhîa's squad had been concealed in one of the hottest deserts and detailed to seek out rebel human groups still holding out in the wilderness."

"Yes Commander!"

"I want to make my … our … stay on Earth as comfortable as possible! I have already asked one of my best engineers to draw up plans for converting the top two floors of the Washington Hilton to a single-floored penthouse for me!"

****

9 weeks until Zero Hour

"Jake. It's Don." The three knocks on my door at midday had been followed by that familiar voice. I let Don in. Neither mobile phones nor telephones worked in Washington any more. The postal service had been patchy and, anyway, the Ischians monitored it so that foot-power had become the only way of getting messages around.

"We found DeTunne," he burst out, as soon as I sat him down on the balcony. As usual, the 'rain' fell in a smothering blanket. The large drops of condensation dripped from my eyebrows on to my nose, then to my mouth and on to the lapel or my shirt, causing a tiny tapping sound. It depressed me even more.

"Where?"

"It wasn't hard. We scoured the doss-houses and there he was. We have him secured. You want to meet him?"

"Not really. Did you mention my name?"

"No … ."

"Good. It would only make him more reticent. *You* question him Don. Dig gently. We need to know if he has access to the outside. Ply him with drink, drugs, whatever he needs … ."

Don stared at me.

"I know. I know. But these are desperate times."

"Okay. You're the boss."

It's been a long time since I heard that!

Don knocked on my door again in the middle of the night. I let him in and he blurted out:

"He buckled. Well, actually he didn't. He was only too happy to spill, once he knew who we were. Ego, I guess … ."

"Well? Don't keep me waiting!"

"Power plant, on the south side. Underground. Disused. Gap in the dome-grid, apparently. Can't stay Jake. I have to go. We're organising a little advanced party to scout it out. You want to come along?"

"Of course!"

He patted me once on the shoulder and left.

***

9 weeks until Zero Hour

We called the circle of generators, creating the highly-charged electrical 'dome' over Washington the dome-grid. Created using Ischian technology, it had been little understood by Engineers in Washington. The process by which the generators had been created, however, *was* now well understood:

First, the Ischians infiltrated the USAC higher political echelons using gold torques, some of them with the receiver's name inscribed in studs of thirty-three carat diamonds.

Soon, they had twenty-two senators, twenty governors, including my friend, Gary Enquine, in California, the Chief Justice, and four other justices of the Supreme Court in their pocket. With these, the aliens were able to get legislation passed to put a defensive perimeter around Washington using a zombie company called Quantrex.

This had been set up only a year before by one of the turned senators.

At this time, USAC held the majority of the newly acquired land taken back from the Rebel forces; the whole of North America, AmericaPol, including the South Polar region, the newly named Austranesia – Australia and Polynesia– some parts of Greater China and Monrussia. They intended to gradually hand back sovereign states as things became more settled. Some parts of Greater China and Monrussia had already been handed back when the alien invasion took place. As a consequence, the population density outside the big North American cities had still be low and the Ischians were able to subjugate the most powerful nation on Earth using just two domes; one over Los Angeles and one over Washington.

***

Chapter Two

9 weeks until Zero Hour

"Watch out for rats! They're the biggest ya ever seen! Must like the humidity!" The southern accent of the urchin, guiding us down the long, disused subway tunnel, seemed as about incongruous as a French accent in Harlem. I looked at his dreadlocks dubiously.

Southern fried King sewer-rat!

DeTunne, with his long, grey-flecked hair now tied back in pony-tail, lurched along behind me and Don brought up the rear.

"Dry DeTunne out! I don't want a drunkard ruining everything!" I instructed Don the last time we spoke. It looked like he hadn't quite succeeded. DeTunne probably had enough spirits in him to last a week!

We had earlier entered at Pentagon City subway station and followed DeTunne down a passenger transit tunnel. DeTunne had looked carefully around him before opening a locked blue door.

"My contact lives in here," he assured us.

We followed DeTunne into a dark tunnel. He stopped and flicked a switch. Two lined of naked bulbs came on, eerily lighting up a dusty dirty tunnel that led on for quite distance. We heard a dog howl.

"Don't worry. That's him!" DeTunne assured us again.

He glanced at my curiously, and then walked on. I wore a scarf which, apart from my eyes, covered my face completely. On top of this I wore an old baseball cap. I deliberately limped, thinking that otherwise DeTunne might recognise something in my motion.

A face appeared in the tunnel. The face had been covered with black soot. The kid with dreadlocks, not more than fifteen, stepped towards us and nodded back over his shoulder.

"Follow me!" he said.

We came to another door. The sewer-rat opened it without a key and we followed him down some steps. A cool blast of air lifted the end of my scarf and slapped it against my face.

"We're in the main tunnel. Be careful now, it's electrified," our guide warned. He turned right and headed down the side of the tunnel. I guessed we were heading south, and not far from the dome-grid.

After walking for five minutes, the sewer-rat crossed the tracks carefully and shone an old, battered, yellow torch on the track rails. They glinted yellow in the torchlight, as if they weren't menacing enough. Gingerly, I stepped over them and then turned to watch the others. I saw that DeTunne seemed completely sober now. I wanted to call out to Don to be careful but managed to keep my mouth shut. Once we were all safely over to the other side, DeTunne continued south. I couldn't see the guide anymore.

"It's just up here," DeTunne whispered. I wasn't sure why he suddenly whispered. We came to an open door in the wall and followed DeTunne through it.

Beyond, I saw a spiral iron staircase. We began to climb.

When I had just become tired enough to want a break, we emerged into a large hallway; dimly lit by lights at various points around the walls and ceiling, perhaps fifty feet above us. I could see machinery everywhere and red warning signs.

"One of the old power stations," said the sewer-rat confidently. "It's disused now, at least by most of Washington. But we still run a generator… to supply power for my community down here." He waited, with the confidence of a tour guide, for this information to sink in. "Over there is the dome-grid. Follow me." We followed him, stepping carefully over patched power cables which sometimes running across concrete, sometimes mesh, floor ways. Our guide stopped. He took an empty beer can from his pocket and tossed it in front of him. It travelled about ten feet before exploding into a tiny fireball. It never landed. Around the small explosion, a shimmering wall, like a sheet of water, became apparent; the dome-grid. I had never been this close.

"Never touch that!" the sewer-rat said, laughing.

He led us to a large gas-turbine generator; I recognised the machinery from some of the plants we had guarded on Io years go. It lay still now.

"We only run it occasionally. It uses too much fuel," our guide said, placing his small hand affectionately on the casing of the turbine. "We use batteries for most of *our* lighting! We *steal* them from above!"

He led us to the front of the turbine, near to the dome-grid.

"Careful!" he said, needlessly, holding up his hand. None of us wanted to get anywhere near the invisible wall. Looking closely, I could see the familiar brown burn mark in a line around the casing. One always saw this where something solid crossed the dome-grid. Eventually, the casing would burn through and would become useless. But somehow, the grid seemed to be able to detect what had already in place on day one and not burn it as much.

"So where's the gap?" asked Don.

"There!" cut in DeTunne, pointing to the floor, by the casing.

"Yeah," the kid confirmed. "When we run it up to full speed, it creates a gap, just by the casing, there. One of my mates found it when he kicked an empty oil can. It passed straight through with no problem."

"Wow!" I said. I bit my lip at my stupid mistake of speaking. DeTunne looked at me and shrugged.

"You have to squeeze right against the casing to get through. Several idiots have lost arms and legs doing this," said our guide.

"Okay. When?" asked Don.

"How many?" the kid asked.

"One. Him," Don replied.

"Two," added DeTunne. "He's not going without me. In any case, I know where to go, once you get through. There are Ischian soldiers all over the place. He will never make it alone."

Don looked at me. He knew I didn't want to spend any time with DeTunne. The ex-USAC man would find out my identity eventually. But he had probably been right. I had a terrible sinking feeling but I nodded.

"Okay. Two," said Don.

"Cost you," replied the kid, grinning.

"How much?"

"Two thousand bucks!"

"Fuck off. DeTunne says you charge him five hundred!"

"He's a trader. Gives us good deals and gets us business. For you it's two grand. Take it or leave it."

Don looked at me again. I nodded. Two grand would be all the money I had but we didn't have time to bargain.

"When?" Don repeated.

"Whenever," the kid said nonchalantly.

"Okay. We'll let you know, through DeTunne."

We retraced our steps and Don and I went back to my apartment. We left DeTunne looking for an open liquor-store in town.

***

9 weeks until Zero Hour

"What are you going to do?" Don asked, after I poured him a glass of bourbon.

"I don't know. I haven't thought this far ahead. Until the other day, I thought there was no way out of here, apart from a direct attack. I *was* thinking about a rebellion. That *was* my plan."

"Yeah. But you always said you wouldn't lead it..."

"That's right. My life is the spiritual one now … . At least it's supposed to be … . Much harder since the death of…"

"Yeah … . But you feel *some sort* of obligation, don't you?"

"Listen, I don't owe the USAC anything anymore! I made sure of that. When I got out, it was a full honourable discharge – no chance of me being called up again. I didn't want *that* hanging over my head!"

"Alright! Alright! So you have said a thousand times. But things have changed. We need you. The *World* needs you! That may sound a little dramatic, but it does! If you can get through to any Rebel group, maybe even the USAC, you can tell them what's going on in here. Who better? And you already effectively organised the group in LA."

"Well, even if I do get out there, where do I go?"

Don stood up and paced around the room. "Finding out about the sewer-rats wasn't the only information we got out of DeTunne. He was quite talkative actually. He told us there is a big Rebel stronghold in Utah; out in the desert somewhere. It even has some ex USAC soldiers and is rumoured to be in contact with the old IM regime – your mates."

"Ha!"

"Anyway he told me something very interesting..."

"Oh? Go on, then. Don't hold back."

"Apparently this group have an old SU 401 … or what's left of it."

I sat bolt upright. "Really? An SU 401?" I stood up. "Now I *am* interested. Can DeTunne get us there?"

"No. Apparently not. Although the sewer-rats have contacts outside who can. DeTunne is just acting in his own interests; doing business with the outside to line his own pockets. He doesn't go far when he goes outside. At least that's what he told me."

"Okay. I'll go … with DeTunne. We must go soon; to-morrow, if possible. I'll need plenty of cash, as much as you can get Don." I paced around the room now, trying to think of everything I needed to take and do once I reached the outside.

***

9 weeks until Zero Hour

DeTunne and I reached the gas turbine generator, just as it reached its maximum rotation speed. The giant fly-wheel, aligned with the dome-grid, had become a blur. A violent hum, almost a scream, emanated from the whole generator. I had to yell at the kid with dreadlocks to make myself heard.

"You going first?"

"Sure. Watch."

For the first time, I noticed the brown blood stains on the floor and casing, over on the other side of the dome-grid. I must have not wanted to see them before.

The sewer-rat drew a tin can from his pocket and threw it through the imaginary gap of the dome-grid. The can passed straight through and went spinning across the floor to end up against a cabinet, outside the grid.

Wow!

The kid lay up against the generator casing. Its vibrations shook him violently but he looked fearless as he wriggled through the gap. He stood up and beckoned me through.

I knelt down and slid my long bag through to him. One of the handles sparked into brief flame, as it touched the field, but the kid stamped it out.

I lay down and pressed myself against the generator. I regretted not keeping myself slimmer. As my neck passed through the gap, my hair stood on end and I could feel, ra-ther than hear, a crackling sound. But moments later, I felt the kid pulling my collar and I kicked against a protrusion

on the generator to push myself through. I stood up, relieved and waited for DeTunne. He passed quickly
though, looking like an old hand. The kid led us away
from the screaming generator and into a side-corridor,
closing the door so we could talk.

"Down here and then down the tunnel for about half a
mile and you will see a door on the right. It says, 'Danger
High Voltage. Risk of death'. And there is a graffiti logo,
our logo. It's a red triangle with a slash… like this." He
mimed a sword cut across his neck, from high on the left
to low on the right. He grinned. "Don't go past this 'cause
you will come to the tunnel entrance. The Ischians always
watch it. Head for Huntley Meadows Park. Follow the
path into the park at the end of Harrison Lane. Somebody
will be waiting for you. Good luck." He opened the door
and left. We reached the park at dusk after dodging Ischian patrols. A tall man stepped out of the bushes and
pointed an X.10 laser at us. My journey, being passed
from one rebel group to another, to Utah, had begun.

***

9 weeks until Zero Hour

Dee-low sat bolt upright in bed. The image filled his
mind; a large tan-coloured seed, bursting with life. Dee
had come to trust his dreams; they usually told him something.

"A seed! That's it! Yes. Why not?"

He rubbed his eyes and put on his headband. Ten years
old, it nevertheless had what Dee still thought as a cool
feature; BPR. Dee still struggled to fully master Brain
Pattern Recognition. He focused hard on the previous
day's record logs, and after a slight pause, up they came
on the lenses in front of his eyes.

Ambi-xjhu's invention had been given an un-pro-
nounceable name in Ischian and the technology still
wasn't known to other humans so Dee had named it the
'temposcope' for now. He scrolled through the pages of

temposcope logs. Suddenly an image flashed up of his ex, Jay, lying naked on a bed.

"Damn! I'll never get the hang of this BPR!"

He concentrated harder and the logs reappeared. He scrolled until he came to the page with the anomaly. In all the hundreds of thousands of logs he had made, this had been the only one with an anomaly. Both he and Ambi-xjhu had, in little more than five years, deduced that the temposcope origin, or date zero, had been sometime around 28,000 years BC, Earth time; just about the time Dee lived in. Beyond this, both had diverged in their re-search. Ambi-xjhu, of course, felt sure, or perhaps hope-ful, that the point of origin in space would be somewhere near Isch-su. Dee approached the problem with a more open mind. Both knew they were looking for an anomaly in the results.

The temposcope received images frozen in time and reflected from surfaces local space. It wasn't a time ma-chine in the sense that you could actually visit the past, but you could catch echoes of it in the form of images on the receiver.

Of course, the novelty of exploring events in one's own past quickly paled. Dee had experienced great diffi-culty in tracking down the exact moment Beethoven cre-ated the opening bars of the Fifth Symphony and the mo-ment Julius Caesar had been assassinated; in reality these events were not nearly as singular as history had painted them, either in time or theatricalality. Dee quickly decided that he would be more interested in finding the origin of time itself. As Ambi-xjhu had taught him, and he had found to be true, the pursuit of God is the pursuit of time.

The temposcope stored each image's digital matrix with another parameter; the Ambi-Low rating. Dee felt particularly proud of this metric's appropriate name; in-ferring the ambiance intensity as well as citing the names of its two inventors. It measured the intensity of the im-age. As one scanned the Universe, or moved back in time on any particular point, one expected each Ambi-Low parameter or AL rating, to be slightly lower than the previous one, in the order of 1×10^{-20} lux.

Ambi-xjhu had hypothesised, and Dee had later concurred, that there could be only two exceptions to this; firstly, an eddy or vortex, where a time-traveller had passed through, arrived or left and secondly, the origin of time itself, if it existed.

Dee had been unable to verify the first condition, since this almost always occurred in deep space and the eddy quickly dissipated. However, he now found himself looking at an anomaly on screen. Not only that but, as he had expected, he could see a progression of decreasing lux suddenly become a progression of increasing lux.

'Shit! It's here!'

Dee threw his headband onto the bed and pushed open the door to his hut. He stood on the small veranda he had built and looked at the verdant hills around him.

Somewhere here is the origin of time.

"Dee! What you doin'?"

The voice from his bed drew him back inside. Kneeling on the bed he kissed his wife. She murmured:

"Um. What ah you going to do today dea'ah?"

"Honey! I am gonna be really busy. And I mean *busy*! I wish I could speak with Ambi-xjhu."

Shihu opened her eyes and smiled at him. Of course, she had aged a lot now, to her late forties. Stone might not even recognise her. But Dee thought her still beautiful.

'And she has the mind of a twenty-one year old! Just like me!'

Her Native American dialect actually seemed closer to the Ischian's language than Dee's own. Consequently, she had no problem extending the vowel in a descending tone, represented by a caret in Ischian script, or using a hard but quiet 'T,' represented by a hyphen.

"How is Ambi-xjhu?" she asked, pronouncing the alien name correctly.

He kissed her again. "I don't know honey. Anyway, I think I may have found something important!"

"What?"

"Tell ya' soon, honey!"

Dee fired up the temposcope with the biggest display and brought up the two logs which held the data for the anomaly. He placed them adjacent to each other. It took the screen nearly a minute to render the first image full-screen. Dee sat back, incredulous. Image quality had never been good, he saw little colour and a lot of grain, but he couldn't mistake the face, looking down at something on the ground, with blue sky behind him.

'Stone!' he thought.

Stone wore the white space suit which had been a few sizes too large.

'It has to be the day they crash-landed!'

Dee's mouth fell open. He tried to form words like 'why' and 'how' but gave in to just staring at the screen. His mind went into overdrive. He had to talk to Stone. No, he had to talk to Ambi-xjhu. Or both.

"But there's no way of contacting Stone!" he told himself.

News never reached Dee directly from Earth's 22nd Century. There would be no direct line of communication back thought the wormhole, even using the latest laser transmission technology, built under license from the Ischians. The last news he had came six weeks before. That had come from Ambi-xjhu, brilliant young Ischian scientist, rebel and student of the great Kek-suîxjh.

Dee had woken one morning a year before, feeling sure somebody had been speaking to him in his sleep.

"Walk with me a little while, my little friend," he recalled the voice saying. *It had sounded older than he, wise, and kind.*

"Where are we going?" he asked, timorously

"You will see. Into my garden. Come, Dee-low."

"How do you know my name?"

"All things are clear, without knowing, when you know the way!" The voice laughed at something.

Dee low had looked across in the half-light to Shihu. She still slept peacefully. He lay back and closed his eyes. For some time, he floated on the edge of sleep, neither dreaming nor thinking. Images flowed through his mind. Then he saw a face; Ambi-xjhu.

"Yes! It's me!" the voice said. "Ambi-xjhu." I am practising the Path of the Universal-mind. Kek-suîxjh taught me!

From that day forward, Ambi-xjhu had contacted Dee frequently using this method. In the last few months, the young alien had kept him updated on Earthly matters. But for some reason, Ambi-xjhu had been silent now for six weeks. Dee knew of no way to initiate a 'conversation.' He felt perplexed, frustrated.

Shihu brought him a beaker of kech. He sat in his favourite wicker chair, taking the hot May sun. The heat, and the sound of insects, intoxicated him. Dee found himself slipping away from his troubled thoughts.

"Ah! Dee! I found you!"

Dee immediately guessed that the voice inside his head had to be Ambi-xjhu.

"I can tell when you want me, if you want me badly enough. What's happening?"

Dee mumbled something in his imperfect attempt at answering using the Path of the Universal-mind. Ambi-xjhu might be a novice, but Dee could be considered a veritable baby. Eventually, after much effort, he formed the sentence:

"I have found the anomaly!"

"An anomaly, you mean?"

"The anomaly!"

"Surely not? Where?"

"Here. On Earth. Now. I will tell you more when I know. Can you contact Stone?"

"Stone? He is on Earth. But I have bad news for you Dee. I didn't want to tell you this and there is nothing you can do about it right now."

"What?"

"Earth has been invaded at last. By the Imperial Fleet. They have sent many ships, including at least one battleship to Earth. Stone's father must have been trapped. Kek-suîxjh hasn't been able to contact him for nearly two of your Earth months."

"Is he dead?"

"No. Kek-suîxjh thinks not."

"And Stone?"

"We don't know. Neither of us has ever communicated with Stone, using the Paths of the Universal-mind. He is a stubborn Banf-haschîsh! Sorry, excuse my language."

***

9 weeks until Zero Hour

Lieutenant Hani Deitner returned to the Operations Room with his detail after just one hour. They had not been able to take the truck far so he felt exhausted. But every last soldier still able to shoot a laser now knew what to do. They knew they had to be at the Hanger in five hours.

"Reporting Colonel. All remaining forces now instructed for retreat!"

"Good work Lieutenant. Now, you better get a few hours' sleep. I am gonna need you fully alert for our exit. Oh, and one other thing; I am going to put you in charge of a squad. That means you now have to record your activities for the Amtel blog."

"Yes, Ma'am! But I thought it had been closed down. Surely there's no subscriber left?"

"That's probably true. Today's will be the last possible entry. The transmitter in the MCS probably wouldn't reach the Moon or any other likely remaining allies, even in peacetime. With the Ischians blocking transmissions, there's no hope. But this will the last chance for all of us to record our last wills and testaments. Even the privates have borrowed sets from commanders to leave theirs. Use the third room on the right. It's Pfenigshaven's. Record your message and get some sleep."

"Yes sir. Sir?"

"What is it?"

"I had an idea."

"Go on. I need any ideas I can get."

"I saw this film, once, a nature film, about a bird which pretended it had a broken wing to avoid predators. I thought that we should deliberately damage the MCS. Take of one of the PODs and make it look like it's been torn off. Then rig the side of the Hanger to blow out. When we slip out quietly, it will look like the MCS has *fallen* out. If we drift for a while, the Ischians may assume it's just a *wreck*."

"Hm. I don't like the thought of losing a POD. But something like that... I will get the engineers on to it. Nice idea Deitner. Sleep well."

Climbing over debris and negotiating the corridor to the Senior Staff quarters, Hani Deitner found the empty cabin and sealed himself inside. He wearily pulled on the Trion head-band and said:

"Record. Hm. This is the log of Lieutenant Hani Deitner June 3, 2136."

He sat staring blankly at the screen for a few moments. His dark brown hair, stubble and goatee made him look like a criminal. Goatees were forbidden in USAC regulations, but since the alien attack the book had been thrown away and discipline had become secondary to survival.

With a deep voice, Hani tried his first words:

"Hello subscribers; on Earth, Mars, the Moon, or wherever you may be now. That is... if any of you *are* left alive. I don't know what to say! I've never done one of these before!"

He laughed nervously.

"I don't have parents or relatives; what replicant does? I had some time with a foster family in New Brooklyn, on the bad side of the Moon dome! Anyway, I doubt they remember me much now. The USAC is my family now. But I joined late. Ran with the mob in Lunar City; stealing hoverbikes, cars, shoplifting – the usual. USAC made me. I don't have anything to leave … I had a collection of lager cans but my bunk got blown to pieces by the Ischian Dogs – should I say that? Oh well, seems a bit late for... protocol. This is going to be a fight to the death. Probably the end for us. Let's see… I think that's it. Oh, and if anybody knows me, I got promoted to Lieutenant!"

He grinned like a stupid kid. Then he said:

"End recording."

He ordered a pizza and lager on the battered n-gen, ate it quietly and then lay on the bed. Occasional sounds of explosions and pinging of live ammunition off some metal surface somewhere had become the lullaby of Deitner's life. They lulled him to sleep now.

Three hours later, another Lieutenant woke him:

"Lieutenant. You're wanted, *now!*"

"Suit up Lieutenant!" Dalgleish bellowed at him. "You take the first detail to the Hanger and set up a perimeter around the MCS."

She strode past, issuing instructions to the officers.

"Yes ma'am!" Hani replied.

Within twenty minutes, having me no resistance, Deitner had led six men to the Hanger deck and dispersed them; some on the gantries, others around the old MCS. It hung from the gantry crane by ten heavy chains. Two of the diesel intakes had been hacked off roughly and one of the crawler-tracks hung off at an angle. Two men worked with blow torches to completely remove it.

'I guess we won't be needing it' thought Deitner.

Six other men were climbing up a ladder to the entrance port, carrying barrels of provisions.

"Twenty minutes to launch!" echoed in the vast bay.

The Museum signs had been removed. Deitner could only guess that the Colonel worried the aliens could read English.

Shots could suddenly be heard far away. Until now, only the sound of the crane's diesel engine and men's voices had filled the bay.

"They're coming!" he yelled to his men. "We must hold this bay!"

The Colonel arrived with the last of the men from the Operations Room, each carrying folders of documents or crates. They clambered into the MCS.

Then the men with the blow torches yelled, "Clear!" and Hani's ears rang from a deafening clang. The crawler-track fell to the steel grid floor.

Slowly, the crane lowered the crippled MCS to the floor, where it tilted drunkenly over to one side.

'We have to go, *now*!' Deitner thought. 'If the Ischian dogs see us before we blow the hanger, we're finished. He stood up and ran to the MCS entrance port.

"Colonel Dalgleish!" he shouted.

"What?"

"We have to go, now! I can hear the dogs. They're getting close!"

"Not yet Lieutenant. We said we would wait for the rest of the men, and we will. If the Ischians catch us, so be it; we all die together."

"Yes, sir."

Come on! Come on! Where are you?

Deitner tried to watch for the enemy but his eyes were really looking for the last grunts. He prayed they would come soon. A large explosion almost rocked him from his feet. The first squad of retreating USAC troops from the upper decks ran on to a gantry, to cheers from Deitner's men. A few other squads started appearing and climbed down to where the old MCS waited silently.

A man ran up to Deitner. "Lieutenant. We came from the highest level. Before we left I could see two of the other squads taken out by the IDs." He suddenly looked sad. "I think we may be the last, sir. The ID's are close behind us. You have a couple of minutes at the most. We left a mine to keep them busy that long. After that..."

"ID's? You mean Ischians?"

"Yeah. We call 'em that – Ischian Dogs. Listen, there's no time!"

"Yeah. I know. Okay. Let's go. Fall back men!"

Deitner led his men and the lone Corporal back to the MCS entry hatch.

"Colonel. The dogs are minutes away. This man says he thinks there are no more squads out there. They left a mine to keep the IDs busy." He wanted to suggest they leave but he bit his tongue.

"ID's?"

"Ischian Dogs ma'am. Not my..."

"Okay. Roll up the ramp! We're going!"

The last men climbed aboard and the crew sealed the entry hatch. The pilot tapped the button to evacuate air from the Hanger and set the anti-grav to neutral.

Slowly, the MCS floated off the deck. With deft blips on the thruster controls, the pilot kept the ship steady. However, the Hanger decks were starting to slide away sickeningly. The station's central systems had been accessed and damaged by the Ischians. It would be only a matter of minutes before the whole station disintegrated.

"Blow the wall now!" the Colonel shouted.

Outside the MCS, the entire side of the Hanger blew out, forced open by carefully placed charges. Black space appeared immediately as the smoke got sucked out.

The pilot manoeuvred the ungainly MCS to slip it through the gap and out into space. All lights were off. To an outsider, the MCS looked to be derelict. Every man on deck held his breath. Slowly, ever so slowly, the old MCS drifted away from Station 5.

***

5 weeks until Zero Hour

A man, with a Mohican-style strip of hair down the centre of his shaved head, sped through the deserts of Utah on a vehicle built before his father had even been a twinkle in *his* father's eye; a black Harley Davidson. A plume of dust marked his path and he checked his mirror continually for patrolling alien cruisers. Since the last rebel checkpoint, where he had been divested of his laser pistol, rifle and helmet, he felt naked. Now, he just wanted to find the headquarters of the legendary Desert Princess, which would mean safety again for him.

"Don't wait up! But keep an open mind." His last message from Dee-low, who had already travelled beyond the rim of the Solar System at 37,000 miles per hour, made him feel empty, as it did every time he thought of it. His friend had gone! He would probably never see Dee again.

Since then, and because he could not follow Dee, there had only been one reasonable thing he could do with his life. Ignoring his mother's entreaties, he had joined millions of other hopeful young men, who were trying to join one of the paltry forces resisting the Ischian invasion. Most couldn't get very far from home. Almost all available transport had been requisitioned by the USAC, who were quickly running out of their own vehicles. He had been lucky. For once, he hadn't *stolen* a cruiser but had stowed away on one of the last black-marketeer ships bound for Rebel strongholds on Earth. There, he had bought the Harley.

"Come *on*! *Come on*! This is like a kid's hover-car!" he yelled at the ancient machine.

The old, chrome-plated speedometer of the Harley indicated 110 mph with the twist-grip throttle against the stop. Stone's cheeks were scalloped by the buffeting air, his tears torn into the slipstream. He pressed his left knuckle into his eye-socket, to clear the moisture so he could see the apparition up ahead more clearly.

"That must be it!"

A single black twist of smoke curled lazily into the laser-blue sky, above a rocky bluff, a few miles ahead and to the left. The old road, giving way to prairie grass in places, led straight as a bolt, past one corner of the bluff. He slowed as he reached the cliffs of sand stone, blushed by the midday sun. He lifted his newly acquired Silver-Classic VisGogs and scanned the side of the road nearest the bluff.

"Here we go!" he thought.

Stone turned off and followed the rutted dirt track which led to the bluff. The Harley's rear tyre bounced and slid sideways as he tried to keep the power down and the bike facing the right way. A man wearing green khakis jumped out into the road, right in front of stone, and brandished a large, green laser. Stone braked and kicked the bike into neutral.

"Kill it!" the sentry yelled, running his index finger across his throat for emphasis. "State your business son," he added, when the motor stopped.

All kinds of stories, anecdotes and fantastic claims to glory ran through Stone's mind but he knew from experience that the Rebels liked everything straight.

"I'm looking to join somebody who is fighting the aliens."

"Oh *really*! We're a little … young, ain't we?" The man spat a wad of chum onto a rock, where it sizzled.

"Well, I first joined the Rebels when I was twelve, I have stolen two cruisers in my time and the second one I took through a worm-hole… and came back."

"Oh *really*! Hah! You're a cocky one, ain't ye!" The sentry balanced the stock of the laser which Stone recognised as a clover leaf, on his hip, and lifted his cap off his sweating forehead before replacing it. "What's your name?"

***

5 weeks until Zero Hour

A senior Ischian scientist and philosopher, Kek-suîxjh had been traveling in space for over one hundred and sixty Ischian years. After finding out that his wife, a senior civil servant in charge of the High Council's security, planned to kill him, he had escaped in a stolen cruiser. His crime? He wanted to find the home planet of the Ischian god, Vîu.

Now, his stolen cruiser followed a trajectory to KL42501; the star he had identified as Vîentxa in Ischian mythology. Here, he believed their god Vîu had set out to populate the Universe and here he hoped to find the answers to many questions. Time had almost become meaningless to Kek-suîxjh on the old K-17 cruiser, which he had named 'Pet Sounds' after the Beach Boys album. Nights and days were the same. He had set the ambient light to dim periodically to simulate artificial night. On most 'days,' he didn't even think about ship's destination. He spent most of his time working at solving problems in his mind. Years ago, Ambi-xjhu had used the PBS beacons to send through plans for his time-echo imager, what the Human, Dee, called the temposcope. Now, Ambi-xjhu had just used the Paths of the Universal-mind to tell Kek-suîxjh that Dee had located *the* anomaly. Dee suggested that the origin of time had been on *Earth*, 30,000 Earth years ago! It seemed preposterous. Kek-suîxjh couldn't accept it. The implications of Dee's suggestion were two-fold; firstly, that time must be an abstract, past and present and that the real Universe is somehow independent of time and secondly, that Humans, and not Ischians, were somehow closer to Vîu, or at least more important.

The first implication derived from the fact that hard evidence *did* exist for life, and the Universe before 30,000 years ago. Thus time must have spread out from its origin; both forward and back. This Kek-suîxjh could accept if he imagined that the Universe to be some kind of whiteboard, imagined into being collectively by all beings as a medium of communication; not a new theory.

The second implication, that Humans were closer to Vîu, Kek-suîxjh could not accept because in almost all ways, Ischians were superior. Kek-suîxjh thought himself a rational, and open-minded, non-racist Ischian, but there it was.

In only one area had the Humans surpassed Ischian science: proving the multi-verse. In the early Human 21st Century, the existence of an elusive particle they called the Higgs boson had been proved. This strengthened the arguments for super-symmetry. This implied, through string-theory, that there were indeed multiple Universes, in parallel with each other; plates if you like.

Ischians too had come up with their own version of string-theory earlier, but constant wars and the destruction of their own planet had hindered their ability to build the vast research centres required to prove the theory.

Kek-suîxjh regretted that the combined Ischian-Human Science Summit, planned by Ambi-xjhu before the High Council had launched war on Earth, had not taken place. Ambi-xjhu planned to shown a recording by Kek-suîxjh, wherein he would propose that the 'whiteboard' be called a Tomoverse; from TMV, Total of Multi-Verses. Kek-suîxjh still felt quite proud of the term.

Kek-suîxjh struggled out of his seat in the lounge of the Pet Sounds. He had been playing through the whole catalogue of Beethoven lately. The excellent Ninth Symphony had just closed.

"The air-quality is getting worse. Soon I will become ill. And I am old! Not good" he muttered to himself.

He stroked his muzzle and long, soft, velvet ears, switched on the PBS transmitter and sent a message to his student:

Dear Ambi-xjhu, my fine student and friend,

I find the idea of Earth as the origin of Vîu's 'time' hard to accept. Please ask the young Dee to recalibrate his TEI, which he calls a temposcope, and take the readings again. I feel there must be some logical explanation for the peculiar readings.
I have made some of my own modifications to the TEI. They are only very slight improvements. I will send you the designs. I have also become aware of strange anomalies in space-time, somewhere far off my starboard bow. It seems that stars there are diverging at a greater rate, while at the same time, slowing their speed away from the Universe's origin. From what we know of the Tomoverse, I am proposing that this might be caused by an interface between our Universe and another; likened to two balloons pressed together, forming a flat disk where they touch. This could force the stars near that interface, which are accelerating towards it, to diverge more quickly and yet slow in speed because of the decreased distance to the edge, or surface, of our Universe. I would hope you would concur. I propose to make a slight detour so that I can pass by this anomaly. I have travelled this far and another few months more will make little difference. I had thought I would reach it in two weeks but now I see that it will be more like four. I hope you are well. Have the Imperial forces been too troublesome? On second thoughts, don't answer that question. I know your ship is on the run. Be careful not to reveal anything of your location in your reply. How is the war on Earth going?
Your teacher, Kek-suîxjh.

A week later, Kek-suîxjh had his reply. It was curt.

> If one travels across all multiverses to the
> origin of them, all you will find something ar-
> tificial and of the making of Man, and Ischian,
> imagination. It will be an answer to nothing –
> Ambi-xjhu.

***

5 weeks until Zero Hour

DeTunne wheeled around at the edge of the precipice.

"I know who you *are*! I *know* that voice. You're Jake *Nanden*, you fucker!"

The sun had just begun to set over the gully in Kansas. Our guide, a young black girl called Tam, had chosen the camp for its view over the countryside all around us. I put down my mug of hot vegetable soup. The game was up. I unrolled the scarf around my face.

"Yes! It's me, DeTunne. Looks like we're gonna have to have this out, one way or the other."

DeTunne pointed his old X.10 at my head. "This time I'm going to *have* to kill you!"

"Hey! Break it up boys! What's this all about!" yelled Tam, jumping to her feet, the coloured wooden beads in her tightly-braided hair making tiny clacking noises as they touched.

"He's a fucking traitor, a callous bastard and a shit, to boot!" yelled DeTunne. "Oh yes, everybody thinks he is a hero, the great Jake Nanden, but I know what he *really* is!"

Tam looked at me.

"Look DeTunne," I replied. "I didn't know about the whole blanker problem... I didn't know about the problems I created for some of you. You say I'm a traitor, that I abandoned replicants, but look at it this way. When I thought I was a replicant, did I consider us less worthy than straight humans?"

Both Lawrence DeTunne and I knew well enough the answer. DeTunne spat on the ground.

"Clever words. Yeah, you did a lot for us, *then*. But what did you do for us *after*? And anyway, that's not why I am gonna to kill you."

"Well, why then?"

"Did you know Jena was a blanker?"

The shock almost made me faint. I couldn't comprehend how the two words 'Jena' and 'blanker' could be connected so nakedly. "Wha-...?"

"Yeah! You bastard. Lincoln dropped her. Oh he bided his time. After you married Katie, Lincoln went to work. He made sure he stripped every asset away from Jena and then he pushed her out. You know why?"

"No?"

"Because he was a replicant! Yeah! Funny, isn't it? None of us knew. But he hated you so *much*, he was prepared to do *anything* to hurt you. I tried to look after her, of course, but in the end, her drug addiction forced her over the edge, into becoming a blanker!" Tears rolled down DeTunne's cheeks. "I loved her!"

"But drugs? She wasn't addicted to any *drugs*!"

"She *was* after Lincoln finished with her."

I had to sit down before my legs went from under me.

"I'm sorry," I said, almost in a whisper.

"It's time to move," said Tam. "Put that gun away, unless you're gonna use it mister!"

DeTunne swore and threw the X.10 to the ground in anger. A spurt of dust hit me in the face.

I had plenty of time for thinking that night. We camped by the precipice; a good vantage point. The air seemed crystal-clear and, apart from the sigh of a gentle breeze and distant cries of a few animals, I only had the crackling of the fire for company. The others had fallen asleep. Soon, even the crackling of the fire became too much for me. I walked to the edge of the precipice and swung my legs over to sit down.

In the back of my mind, I began to wonder what Gary Enquine might be up to in Los Angeles. I had never given up on the friend who had never given up on me. It had been I who had warned Adam and his wife Darda not to use the torques when I knew they had been gifts from an Ischian. They had been able to cast them away but I had no idea if Gary had. From Tam, I had quickly learned that Los Angeles had been the only other city in the United States of America and Canada covered by an alien dome. New York had been left to the Rebels, since it had little mineral value.

Gary had, of course, been heavily implicated in the conspiracy to put domes over both cities. Quantrex put a perimeter of high-powered, super-cooled magnetic coils around Washington and Los Angeles at an apparent enormous cost which, as it turned out, had been, where necessary, siphoned off from the USAC black budget. There were many questions asked in Congress when the costs escalated but the Senate, upper and lower, were swayed by the argument, from the various senators, governors and law makers implicated later in the conspiracy, that alien invasion had become imminent. The coils could generate laser trajectories upwards which, using quantum diffraction, could be curved to effectively form a protective cone over Washington. At the same time, any beam could detach and shoot down any attacking ship with no loss to the integrity of the dome; a beautifully efficient system.

We *didn't* know, at first, that the beams also worked equally well underground. When the lasers were turned on, nobody could get in or out of Washington, even using the warren of old underground tunnels. We were effectively blockaded.

With Washington as their hostage, the turned politicians announced a break-away democratic party called the New Democracy Union, NDU, who intended, using technology they had acquired from the aliens, to move USAC towards a political system more like that of medieval Europe. They didn't need to. They used their leverage to recruit, and turn, other senators and political leaders in all other states of free or non-rebel nations. Domes were built in these cities too, until the aliens had the means to trap citizens in most major cities, leaving little else but waste land.

Of course, the populace rose in uproar, especially when the climate within cities became hotter, and hotter, to accommodate the needs of arriving aliens and their cohorts. Reaching almost 120 degrees Fahrenheit at midday, it became so debilitating that it helped ground down the populace's will to resist the invasion. Nevertheless, some distress messages did reach USAC and other forces in space, and of course the Lunar Cities and J stations. Forces began to move towards Earth, to rescue its citizens. They were thwarted by the arrival of hundreds of Ischian cruisers; light fighting ships which broke from their space-jumps somewhere near the orbit of Mars. These deployed quickly enough for twenty to take up station around the earth's equator and four each at the poles. From these, and from the huge ship over the North Pole, 100,000 Bekians were transported to earth in shuttles to become the overseers of Earth's people, who were themselves to become slaves. Very few Rebel ships were now able to leave or enter Earth's atmosphere.

At least I had time to help Gary organise some kind of resistance in LA, but I wondered just how far this had advanced.

***

5 weeks until Zero Hour
Stone sighed when the sentry asked his name. He leaned close to the man and whispered in his ear. The sentry's eyebrows jumped.
"No relation of *the* Jake Nanden?"
Stone lied. "Nope!"

"Pity. That might have meant *something*. Tell you what, I might let you pass; you look harmless enough. The old bitch might even find some use for you but you might have to give me a little something for the favour." Seeing the suddenly defiant look in the stranger's eye, he added, "It's either that or you turn right round and go back the way you came."

Stone reached inside his sim-leather jacket and took out a large packet of chum. He tossed it to the open hand of the sentry. "Nice. Maybe not such a dumb-ass kid after all. *And...*"

With a sigh of exasperation, stone chucked the man his chum-pipe, hand-made for him in silver and ebony.

"Whew!" the man whistled. "Getting there..."

"Jesus!"

Stone leaned the bike on its side-stand and pulled his boot off. He pulled out a tiny wad of paper, folded it out to reveal a tatty thousand dollar bill and slapped the bill into the waiting hand, before putting his boot back on.

"Okay! On your way. And good-day to ye' sir!"

Stone gunned the engine, sending a cloud of dirt from the back wheel into the face of the sentry, before riding off.

"Fuckin' creep!" he shouted.

"Mind yer language! Ha! Ha!"

Stone steered the bucking Harley up the mud-rutted track, often standing on the foot-rest to keep his balance, until he reached the top of the bluff. Another green-clad soldier stepped in front of him, holding up the flat of his palm. A second soldier aimed a large laser at Stone's face as he slid to a halt. He killed the engine:

"I've come to fight with the Princess!"

"Yeah! Danny radioed ahead. Here is as far as you go on that thing! It's ours now. Sorry!"

Stone only hesitated for only a moment.

Stolen anyway!

He swung his leg over the saddle and threw the keys to the woman, who looked taller and leaner than the other sentry. She wasn't much older than Stone, had a shaved head and a snake-tattoo on her cheek.

"Name?" asked the woman.

"You know that!"

"Just checking! Come with me."

They topped the ridge and started down the dirt track into a wide valley beyond, enclosed on the far side by another row of hills.

"Where's the camp?" Stone asked. "I can't see nothing, except…" He took off the cheap VisGogs, which cut out too much of the light. "Except that run-down old farm down there and a few dried up fields. Is that *it*?"

"Ha! Nope."

"Where is it then?"

"You're looking at it!" Stone shook his head, incredulous, but followed the woman as they trudged, under the burning sun, down into the valley.

"Could murder a drink... of anything. Got some water?" They were approaching an improbably straight line of fruit trees but even the promise of shade didn't ease Stone's pounding head.

"Wait!" the rebel guard told him.

They passed through the line of trees and Stone looked up. He laughed:

"Nice one!"

Above Stone, a vast expanse of camouflage netting hung between the top of line upon line of fecund fruit trees. Their branches were heavy with heavy, ripe fruit, the like of which he had never seen; succulent oranges the size of grapefruits and plums bigger than most apples in documentaries on J5. Under the first line of trees, ran a long clay pipe, from which water trickled along aisles of irrigation channels into the valley.

"Is it clean? Can I drink it?"

"Sure can! It comes straight from a spring, halfway up the bluff."

Stone cupped a mouthful of the clean, clear water. "Ah! That's good!" He threw some water over the back of his hot neck, immediately easing the throbbing pain at the base of his skull. Following the soldier down the aisles of trees, he emerged into the concealed Rebel stronghold within two minutes.

"Name's Ryan!" said the woman, stretching out her hand. It wasn't taken. "Ha! Wasn't sure about you, at first."

***

5 weeks until Zero Hour

Commander A-schian'bakî had been trained in political, as well as military, tactics and knew the easiest way to subdue the remaining rebel forces on Earth would be to form a pseudo-alliance with their leader. Of course, it would really be a form of slavery but the stupid humans wouldn't realise that until too late. Unfortunately, there *seemed to be* no real single leader of the Rebels on Earth. The old Rebel Alliance had become too fragmented so that now there were many and *very* loosely affiliated Rebel groups. However, she knew of one leader, head of the largest group, who had a particularly strong hold over all who heard of that group. And this leader was female. Her camp lay in an area of desert and A-schian'bakî had positioned her top grunt there. She believed the time to finally be right. She issued a command for her favourite, An-Hnadhîa, to move in on the rebel camp.

"At last! Some action!" An-Hnadhîa grunted

He turned to his 2IC on the bridge of the J-Crawler.

"They don't think we know where they are," he continued, "and, what's more, they don't know we're here. It should be a bloodbath, for them! Ha!"

"Yes sir!"

"We move in at midday. The hotter the better. Remember Ridge A from our briefings?"

"Sir!"

"I want you to move the J-Crawler there so that we can give covering fire to the first troops in. I will go with the second wave. I will be in my quarters, preparing, so..." He patted his 2IC on the shoulder. "Make it smooth!"

The J-Crawler's nuclear motors spun into life. The cloaking camouflage automatically adjusted to depict the illusion of a small human civilian off-road vehicle, showing corrected views from all four sides. The Ischians were becoming very good at bending light to create effective cloaks or invisibility shields.

"Much better than the humans!" the 2IC declared proudly to the small Ischian male driver.

"Yeah. But we still have to un-excavate ourselves, don't we?" the driver said wryly.

The 2IC grimaced at the audacious cynicism of the young driver. He disliked the driver and would have liked to discipline him. He replied:

"Well. Do you know of a better way to stay totally hidden from radar… and all other known means of detection?" His impatience showed in his voice, which irritated the 2IC even further.

The driver pressed a button and the excavator system, modelled on that of captured USAC systems, cut in. The vibration almost shook the canines from the grunts' jaws as the tracks started to in-fill the trench containing the J-Crawler. At the same time, fans blasted away the covering dust of the Utah desert. After a gut-shaking ten minutes, the giant crawler tracks were on a level with the desert around it. Pushing it into first gear, the driver steered for Ridge A, indicated on his blue radar screen.

***

5 weeks until Zero Hour

Travelling by night, sometimes by car and sometimes on foot and keeping to isolated tracks which only Tam seemed to know, we reached the Utah desert without incident.

I tried to form a plan in my head but my thoughts constantly drifted to my family; Katie, my mother and Stone.

Stone had been living in Lunar City. He abandoned the idea of becoming a pilot or journalist and instead embarked on a career in politics. He had been in his final year of a Politics and History Degree on the Moon. I hoped that Stone would have had good enough contacts to escape, somehow. He had probably made it to Earth, *if* he had survived the first attack. I knew that J5 had now been taken out.

All three of us walked, strung out in a line, across a flat stretch of bone-dry ground. DeTunne had mellowed towards me since the fight on the ridge but he still seemed sullen. He turned to face me:

"Where's your habit now, Nanden?"

"Which one? I still like to drink?"

He revealed his teeth with a big grin and suddenly guffawed.

"Ha! Funny. I dunno, maybe you haven't changed, after all." He turned and continued walking.

"Wait!" I shouted. Both Tam and DeTunne stopped. Behind a rock, I peeled off my habit, which concealed a T-shirt and jeans. These had been making me sweat too much anyway so I stripped them off and put on just the dark brown habit of my faith. "There!"

"Ah! The monk! See Tam, this is who he really is! He was a great soldier once; famous across the whole Solar System. Now he's a monk! Ha!" But there didn't seem to be any bitterness in his joke.

"Tam," I shouted. "How come you're still guiding us? Until we reached your group, we had about four guides. But since them, only you?"

"I wanted to leave. I don't care where I go. I just wanted to get away."

"Why?"

"Raped five times in the last year? Do I need to say more?"

***

5 weeks until Zero Hour

In the J-Crawler, An-Hnadhîa watched the green screen over the shoulder of his armaments officer. An-Hnadhîa noticed some red, jagged lines on the screen.

"What are those?"

"Can't tell sir. Some kind of anomaly, under the surface. Could be caves. We've seen plenty of them out here."

"Hm. Nothing unusual then?"

"No sir."

"Alright. Prepare to move forward."

His 2IC, Mrek-anan came to stand behind him. An-Hnadhîa could sense the presence of a nervous Ischian male, too nervous to even get his attention much of the time. He swung round.

"Yes?" he barked.

"We are progressing well, sir. Resistance, so far, has been weak. Casualties light."

"Very good. Now we move in for the final kill, figuratively speaking, of course." He grinned. "Don't forget our orders; the Earth female leader, Princess Muna, or whatever she is called, *must* be taken alive. If any of my soldiers harms a single hair of her pelt, I will have him executed. It will be far worse if she is killed. Remind the troops!"

"Yes, sir!"

***

Chapter Three

5 weeks until Zero Hour
"Looks like Ischian lasers to me. We don't have anything that bright, that powerful," I said, looking at the bright beam and explosions ahead.

"Over the Rebel camp, I reckon," added Tam.

"How far is it now?" I asked.

"Six hours… perhaps a bit more."

"Come on!" I shouted.

I broke into a jog and the others followed. We reached the remains of the camp in three hours. DeTunne, the least fit, followed us in, panting hard.

To my amazement, I saw ground littered with the bodies of dead Ischian males, most of them still in their suits. Many of the Rebels were cataloguing and stockpiling Ishian weapons, which pleased me. Tam spoke to a man, co-ordinating the moving of the rebel wounded:

"Please take us to Muna."

"Who are you?" he replied.

"I'm a Rebel courier. This is Jake Nanden."

"I dunno who *he is* but … . Well... wait, that name sounds familiar. Wasn't he some kind of cool dude in the USAC, years ago?"

I grinned like an idiot.

We were led to a makeshift tent, two ripped sheets tied together and draped over a stick frame, in the centre of the carnage. Out of this, stepped a blonde woman with a sheet wrapped around her shoulders.

The soldier introduced us by whispering in her ear.

"The great Jake Nanden!" Muna said, beaming and extending her hand.

"Well, not as great as *you're* going to be, after news of this gets around, Muna. I've heard of you, *everyone* has heard of the Princess in the Desert, but this is a great victory. You are the first leader to beat the Ischians in a battle … as far as I know. How the *hell* did you do it?"

"They were stupid. We were lucky. Even so, we have suffered terrible losses. There is less than quarter of our original number left. As you can see, it's going to take some cleaning up. I can't speak to you now, though I have no doubt you must have interesting news. I have to organise things here. Denning, give them something to eat and a place to rest." She turned back to me. "I will speak later this evening." She turned away and then turned back. "Oh, there is somebody here you will be glad to meet." With that, she left.

Long after the sun had set, we were summoned to Muna's tent. When we entered, a man sat with his back to us, talking with the great warrior princess. He heard our footsteps and turned. I saw my son.

"Stone! You're alive!" I rushed up to Stone and grabbed him into my arms. He grasped me back. I fought back the tears which he would have thought unseemly in such company. "I thought you were dead! Oh, thank God, figuratively speaking, of course."

"Dad," Stone said, drolly. "You haven't changed. So what god do you believe in now?"

"Ha!"

"I was just saying to your son … ." interjected Muna, "… that he has great leadership qualities *himself*. I heard that he had led several charges, which killed Ischians, and had found a weakness, a point on their armour that affected their Environmental Cycler unit. It might possibly be what turned the battle in our favour."

"Actually, that's not quite true," Stone said. "It was another man who found the weakness. Or at least, he told me about i … . He's dead, now."

"Honesty too!" Muna replied.

I beamed with pride and shook Stone's hand.

"Now, what can we do for you *Jake Nanden*?" Muna asked.

She sat down in a large chair and offering us food and beverages with a flick of her hand.

"I hear you have an SU 401. I would like to borrow it."

Muna looked at me calmly for a moment. Then she threw back her head and laughed. Her laugh came full-bellied and edged with the roughness of a heavy smoker.

"I see. Well, I expected you to be bold... By the way, what are you doing wearing a monk's habit?"

I had to clear my throat for what would not be an easy explanation:

"Well, after I left the USAC, at my own request, I bummed around a while, looking for some worthy cause to champion while still making enough money to support my growing family. Katie, my wife, was still in USAC as a pilot so we weren't poor. Then I found out about a … religious sect, or *cult*, if you prefer, called the Blue Path. I felt curious but sceptical. It was only years later that a mate of mine recruited me. Now, I'm a full-time member, an adept actually, so I make it my business to travel around, looking for … potential new members … ."

"You're an evangelist!" Muna exclaimed.

"No. No, not an evangelist. I don't see it that way. We are very sensitive to whether somebody is ready, and I mean really ready, to take to the Path. But I must admit, the training I have received has not been my first experience of contact with the minds of others..."

My voice must have trailed off as my mind drifted. Jake coughed politely and I refocused on the present. Muna looked at me long and hard. Her eyes had the deeply penetrating perception of somebody twice her age.

"I can see we have much to talk about … later. But to return to the SU 401. Firstly, it's a wreck! It hasn't flown in nearly twenty years! I'm not sure if it will ever fly *again*. Secondly, even if it did fly, what would you do with it?"

I lay back on a large cushion and wondered what to tell them. There would be only so much I could reveal. I started with a question, partly to give me time to think:

"Are you in touch with what's left of the Rebel Alliance Muna?"

"Oh there's plenty of it left alright; fragmented but it's there. My brother is with them now. Of course, nothing has got through to either the Moon or Mars recently..."

"But you *are* in touch. So what do we know of the Ischian forces and what is left of ours? And more importantly, where *are* they?"

Now, *Muna* became hesitant. "Hm. Well, there are a few ships strung out between here and Mars, mostly trying to stay out of sight, hiding behind moons, that sort of thing. Mostly our forces, such as they are, are grouping around the Mars station. But there is really nobody in command. The Commander of S.4, the last I heard, was reluctant to group all his forces there, for fear of an Ischian attack. One more all-out attack by them and we would have nothing left. It's pretty chaotic... And of course there's really not much left on Earth."

We all nodded.

"Of the aliens, all I know is that they have one great ship somewhere over the pole, that's where most of their ground troops came from, and of course they have these domes over Washington and Los Angeles. There have been rumours lately of a rebellion in Los Angeles but no more resistance than that."

"I came out of Washington," I said. "There's no resistance there, yet. But it seems I have a little more information than you … ."

All three of the other guests watched my face curiously. I didn't want reveal any more yet but I had no choice.

"That great ship over the pole; it has a twin. The twin will be arriving in the next few weeks to take up position over the other pole. And later, there will be more. These will circle the equator so that they can set up a field, like the ones over the cities, around the whole Earth. Even with just two ships, they can create a crude version of the dome. But when they have all of them, there will be no escape. They can do what they like with the atmosphere...”

“How do you know this?” asked DeTunne. Stone nodded.

“Yes. How?” asked Muna.

“I was afraid you were going to ask that.”

While I cleared my throat, Stone picked up a bunch of grapes and started picking them off, one by one. I could see he relished his father being put on the spot.

“There is, as I mentioned, an aspect of the Blue Path which I was aware of before I even joined, although I did not understand it at the *time*. Before you were born, Stone, I started hearing a voice in my head. It sounded strange, authoritative and yet kind, and not of my own making. At first I tried to ignore it but it has gone on for many years. Now, I know it to be the voice of an Ischian. His name is Kek-suîxjh.”

Muna eyebrows rose. She looked sceptical

“Now, I know what you’re thinking... But remember there were once benevolent Ischians and, in fact, there is a faction, political in its organisation but actually religiously based, which did not want the invasion of Earth. They are peace-loving and practice something called the Paths of the Universal-mind.”

The faces around me quiesced into confused nods.

“Kek has been keeping me up to date and has found out through his own sources that this attack is coming. He is in touch with a former student of his called Ambi-xjhu, who himself is in touch with Dee. Stone?”

Stone looked up from his grapes. “Huh? You mean using this mind-thing?”

“Yes.”

"Sounds like a load of bollocks to me. Why hasn't he tried to talk to me then?"

"Can we talk about that later?"

"What is this Blue Path anyway?" interjected Muna.

"Please can we discuss that later, too?" I asked.

"Hm. Okay…" she replied. "So you still haven't answered the question; what do you intend to do with the SU 401?"

"What you have told me is as I feared; our forces are dispersed and nobody is really in command. I need to get up there and find somebody to take command. We know that a second battleship will arrive over the South Pole soon. I have other information about the attack that will help us coordinate our response. I have been thinking a lot about what this response should be. I think the only way to effectively fight back is to take one of these battleships. Ultimately, if we don't do that, they will have us in a noose. And negotiation is out of the question."

"Why don't your friendly Ischians help you?" asked Muna

"They are too weak and too few. Kek himself is in exile and on board a ship heading out into deep space."

"If you can communicate with them, why can't your friends help you build a weapon to counter the Ischians?" DeTunne asked.

"We could but it would take too long. There isn't any time."

"But they could help you plan an attack on the battleships?" Stone offered.

"Yes. That's a possibility. Both of them are scientists and of the highest calibre. They might possibly know things about the battle ships which could help us. I can't be sure. They are not familiar with our weaponry. We need to launch some probe attacks ourselves, to find their weaknesses."

"Seems to me like it might be you taking command, Jake Nanden!" Muna said.

"No. I have taken vows of non-violence and also some that mean I cannot impose my will on others. I can't see how it could possibly be me."

"Even if the world needs you?" asked DeTunne.

I smiled and shook my head.

***

5 weeks until Zero Hour

Later, in the tent, Stone told DeTunne and I how he had found the camp; how he had heard of it, acquired a Harley Davidson and how he had reached the camp. He told us what had happened next.

In a calm quiet voice, one I had never heard him speaking with before, he began:

"I had to kick my heels, sleeping in a dusty hut with other fledgling recruits for three days, before Muna would see me. This Rebel called Ryan visited me several times and explained that the Princess met all new recruits before assigning them roles. None were turned away, although a few spies had been immediately executed once discovered. I have to tell you that when I met Ryan, I had a feeling of Déjà vu; like I had met her before. I felt *that* when I met Muna and during the whole battle. I have felt it before.

"I came before the Princess late at night, having been woken from an uneasy sleep. At last, I stood before her in a large tent. She reclined on a large, leather-bound chair, dressed in nothing more than a red, see-through night gown. I think she enjoyed the effect the sight had on me because her smile looked slightly, well, lascivious..."

"Big words, Stone," I interceded.

"Don't interrupt if you want to hear all of it. I haven't quite forgotten my journalistic aspirations! I thought; Phew! This is one intelligent woman! Better watch myself. 'Hello' I said. 'Hell-*o*,' she purred.

"Even reclining, I could see that she was tall. She was blonde, elegant, with a full figure; gorgeous!

"She asked me why I wasn't relaxed or something like that. I said I was and that she wasn't what I had expected. 'What *did* you expect?' she asked me. Of course, I told her that rumours told of a barbarian Princess. I also got very embarrassed 'cause I *now* felt I had to tell her that the rumours also said she rode into battle topless! Funny how some people compel you to say more than you want to…

"She told me some stuff about how war is tough and… oh year, then she asked about my name… I waited for her to comment about you, dad, but she hadn't heard of you! Ha! She told me about her brother and then gave me my first *real* orange and a beer.

"She told me about her name; that her mum … in Mexico … wanted to name her after the moon but her dad had like Muna; which means 'hope,' or something, in Arabic.

"She asked what I was good at, I told her I was the best pilot at the Academy and then that was basically it. But then she made the mistake of asking me if I had another question. And I made the mistake of asking her why she was called the 'Princess.' Something about her brother telling her they were descended from Swedish royalty or something. In fact, a lot of things seemed to come down to her brother!

"I went back to my tent. I slept and next morning I was sharply woken. I heard the shouting only an instant before I heard the explosion. 'What's going on?' I shouted to a man passing my tent. 'Attack! Aliens! Grab a gun – anything!'

"I looked around but could see no weapons, so I ran after him. Soon. I was part of a crowd, running towards the eastern edge of the vast camp. Another explosion ripped the sky apart ahead, momentarily blinding me.

"'Hey, Stone! Follow me,' called a familiar voice; Ryan. As we neared the edge of the camp, I noticed many strange vehicles, all different, being started. Some had large, ex-military lasers mounted on top, others, rocket-launchers. 'Don't worry!' Ryan shouted over her shoulder. We planned this, although it's a bit sudden. The main problem is shortage of weapons. Should be able to find you something soon, though …'

"The rebel camp lay sandwiched between one high ridge, over which I had first approached the camp, and another. Both rose to meet each other in the south west, creating an impassable wall at that end. The two ridges ran north east and slightly away from each other until they formed a wide valley. Shallow ridges crossed this in places. On top of one of these, in the distance, I saw the source of the Ischian firepower; a large crawler of a type I hadn't seen before, its large laser barrel pointing directly at the camp. On each ridge, and moving quickly towards the camp, were hundreds of Ischians, ten feet tall; like men with dog's heads. Each had one of those nasty laser-rifles of theirs and some wore very tight, black suits. I thought; this is going to be the charge of the bloody Light Brigade!

"We emerged from the camp, into an area of low scrub, criss-crossed with shallow gullies. We were part of a large group of rebels making for a slightly higher ridge about half way to the alien crawler, where there were a few stunted trees, the only cover in the valley.

"I turned to see the whole camp rushing towards the attackers. At the rear, were lines of strange armed vehicles and, right in the centre, trailing a plume of yellow dust, I saw one large vehicle with a single figure, standing high on a platform. Even at this distance, her mane of long blonde hair was clearly visible. She was defiantly naked from the waist up, apart from plate armour on the outside of her arms and a large steel helmet. She brandished a combined laser-sword.

"I felt a rising anger because the aliens were attacking Muna. The attack felt personal. 'In here!' Ryan shouted, diving into a depression, formed by a shell explosions.

Bits of bodies and two broken weapons lay around us. Ryan aimed her laser at an alien running towards us at colossal speed. The beam hit the ten foot monster square on the chest but seemed to bounce off. 'Damn!' Ryan shouted. I told her I needed a weapon but she just pointed to a ridge and we ran for it. Gasping, I threw myself against the bank of the ridge when we finally made it. There was plenty of incoming and we were covered with bits of bodies. I… I er… picked a forearm, torn at both ends, from my face and retched. I had no time to be properly sick though. Two other mutilated bodies flew over my head and landed with a sickening wet sound behind me.

"An instant later a human hand appeared over the ridge and a man crawled over, falling between us. His legs were both blown off at the knees. His eyes were wide horror. I knelt beside him. 'Water!' the man mumbled. Then he looked up at the sky, mumbled something else and died.

"That's when I started shaking. 'We're being massacred!' Ryan shouted. 'Take his weapon!' I picked up the old X.50. The moment my sight was trained on a running Ischian, I felt calm again. I fired. The laser shot simply bounced off the alien's black armour, which shone in the sun.

"As you know, the Ischian helmets completely enclosed their heads, including their long snouts. Filters keep the temperature and nitrogen levels inside the Environment Cycler at the right levels for them to fight efficiently but still allowed them to exploit their superior senses. I speculated that these might be weak points in their armour. The Ischian was looking for the source of the near miss. I took careful aim and fired at the nose of the ten foot beast. I gently squeezed the trigger and fired. The alien turned his head towards me at the last moment and the beam of white light missed by an inch. Pissed me off, I can tell you!

"The alien had located the direction of fire and ran towards us. I had just enough time to yell, 'Ryan!' before the huge black shape leaped right over us, landing with a thudding crunch over twenty feet behind. The alien had missed us. He kept running. I twisted and laid back against the dirt bank, fuc-… I mean, bloody relieved, *I* can tell you! 'I think our time has come,' Ryan shouted. She shouted something about looking for a red cord in the dirt. I didn't know what the hell she was on about but she pointed again at the sand so I dug! Not believing for a moment I would, I suddenly clutched something. I pulled it up. It was red. I yanked it and found that it was attached to a large wooden cover. As I pulled, the desert dirt fell away and the cover slowly lifted up. Underneath were stairs.

"Ryan told me to run down the stairs, before standing up. She held her hands above her head in a large 'V' shape. Other rebels stood up and started making their way towards her, dodging shells from the Crawler and laser fire. I turned to look where I expected most of the rebel vehicles to be. I could see none in the dust storm, kicked up by the battle. My last sight of the battle was of a rebel jumping over the ridge next to Ryan.

"Running down a dirt tunnel, which was dimly lit by led lights, I reached a junction and saw a sign which read 'This Way.' I turned right. The tunnel ran straight for a distance before passing other tunnels on the right and left. From those, other rebels emerged and turned into the tunnel, running ahead of me. Soon the tunnel began to rise, now filled with rebels, many wounded, all struggling up the increasing incline. Some whispered or shouted, but many were silent.

"I came to the back of a queue. Men were shuffling forward. Then we reached some steps, roughly cut into stone. Now the tunnel walls were cool and smooth to the touch. I guessed they were in the hills to the side of the valley. We climbed for what seemed an hour. I felt out of breath by the time I finally reached a large open space – a cave. Here, several other tunnels emptied out and the cave filled with about two hundred men. One leader stood at the entrance, shouting instructions. 'Next group of twenty men, step forward! Wait!' he yelled. I joined the back of the short queue. 'Now! Turn to the left and spread out,' he yelled. 'Work towards the cliff. Push 'em off if you have to! Go!'

"I followed the man in front of him, up a short set of rock-cut steps, and out onto the plateau. The man turned left, following others as they sped across the rim of the valley. To our left, several aliens returned fire. The Ischians had their backs to the cliff edge. The battle still raged in the desert, far below.

"I saw how ingenious Muna had been in planning their defence; now we outflanked the aliens who had outflanked us before. My heart lifted. I followed other rebels, who were charging the nearest Ischian with lasers blazing. 'Aim for the small red button on their chest. It's a control for their ECs. It's a weakness!' A man yelled, shooting from behind a rock. A brilliant white beam from the Ischian's laser just missed my ear, singing my hair. I flung myself behind a pile of rocks. My X.50 felt hot and was down to its last few charges. I let it cool for a few moments before placing the barrel in a crevice between two small rocks. I could see the alien clearly, standing his ground and firing at every target he, or it, could see. I thought; so cocky! Bloody fucker!

"I tried to aim for the small red button on the environmental pack strapped to the front of the alien's suit. The small control button made an almost impossible target; about one inch in diameter and moving constantly as the alien swung this way and that, looking for targets. More than ten times, I had been about to fire when the target slipped out of my sights once more. I thought; if I don't get it, nobody will!

"Suddenly the alien stopped firing. It was as if he was listening to something. I fired. The alien's EC pack exploded after an electrical short-out. The alien staggered for a moment but then commenced firing again. I thought; Damn! The fucker is too tough. But the Ischian's aim seemed to be off and after a few more shots, he staggered and then fell to his knees. Now is the time, I thought. 'Jump him!' I shouted. I ran towards the great beast and jumped on the sprawling giant. Its hands were twice the size of my head, it's feet three times. At one moment, it gripped my head in its hand and twisted it. I thought his neck would break but then the alien let go. 'Over the edge with it!' I shouted. Together, we heaved. With barely any struggle, the alien toppled over the edge of the cliff and bounced off the rocks as he fell to his death on the desert below. I told the men around me to help others, pointed towards the head of the valley and looked around me. Only three of the original twenty men were left alive. The man with the information about the EC control was dead.

"I picked up his weapon and ran after the others. We passed several pockets of rebels, each fighting an alien attacker. I passed on the valuable Intel about the Ischian suit weakness and, where we could, we helped. We passed close to the edge of the cliff between two groups and I stopped to look down on the main battle. There was less dust now. I could see that all the Rebel vehicles were stationary and felt a pang of fear. Then, as I watched, the J-Crawler mounted a rise and arrived in the middle of the battlefield. It stopped only yards from Muna's burned-out vehicle. As I watched, there was an almighty flash of orange and both the J-crawler and the Rebel vehicles disappeared in one huge explosion.

"My jaw dropped open, and then I shouted. 'Muna!' For one moment, I thought she was dead. But then the cry went up. Men shouted 'Muna!' as if were a victory and the shouts grew into a chant, carried on by *all* the Rebels.

'She's not dead!' a veteran Rebel said, clapping me on the shoulders.

"I found myself walking calmly back towards a narrow track at the head of the valley, which I saw led down to the camp. Almost all the aliens were dead now; an occasion shot lit up the afternoon sky. Only now did I know how hot, sweaty and exhausted I was.

"When I reached the camp, I volunteered to go out on to the field to find survivors. I worked my way towards the ridge where I last saw Ryan. I finally reached it after carrying three survivors to waiting medical vehicles. I found Ryan laying in the dirt, one arm hanging on by only a few tendons. I knelt beside her. She opened her eyes. 'Stone. You're okay. I wondered; did we win?' I told her we won and that I would get help. I *told* her to hang on! But she grabbed my arm and whispered, 'Nah. No point. Look!' She pulled back her bloody T-shirt to reveal an immense wound in her chest. I could have put my whole fist inside it. I knew she would die. For a moment, I thought of lying but I sat down and she asked me to roll her a chum spliff. She started to say something when she took a drag but I didn't hear her. When I asked her what she said, I saw that she was *dead*. I picked her up gently and carried her to a medical vehicle. When the medics took her, I took the spliff from her mouth and smoked the rest of it myself. I returned to the camp and lay down in the shade of a tree until I heard somebody calling my name. That's when I came to Muna's tent and met you!"

"You tell a good story Stone!" I said.

"Yeah!" added DeTunne.

"You tell a good story, Stone!" DeTunne said.

I said nothing. I felt that, somehow, Stone had already experienced almost as much of life as I had.

***

5 weeks until Zero Hour

A-schian'bakî turned to her 2IC. She had lost not only a battle but her favourite too. Her mood had turned foul.

She barked, "Take us to a point right above that dust-bitch's camp, *now*!"

With just a nod, the 2IC went into overdrive, issuing instructions to every crew member on the vast bridge of the Lu-kshîa in a loud, clipped bark. Each crew-member's ears pricked, listening for the sound of their name or a command which might be for them.

A-schian'bakî continued to stare out of the viewing port, down at the desert of Utah, while the great battleship quickly approached its target.

Now calm, the 2IC said, "We will be directly over their base in approximately seven minutes and twenty-three seconds!"

A-schian'bakî snarled, "I want every camp around hers destroyed, up to a range of fifty miles!" Her voice carried the sound of extreme malice.

"Yes Commander."

The 2IC issued the command and the Weapons Officer ordered his small team to align the giant lasers on the correct co-ordinates.

"Ready!" the Weapons Officer called.

"Do it!" A-schian'bakî barked.

The 2IC nodded and turned to the weapons officer, who needed no more command than a blink to fire.

Twenty two giant white beams stretched out from the great battleship, down to points on the desert floor of Utah. In just ten seconds, 35,000 rebels were vapourised.

***

5 weeks until Zero Hour

We were guests of Muna during the following evening.

"Muna! Muna! Come quick!" a voice shouted from outside the tent. Muna stood up and pushed aside the tent-flap. Immediately we could see that the night sky had been lit up by giant white beams of light. I stood up and rushed to the tent flap.

"What the fuck!" shouted DeTunne.

"Must be Ischian," I said. "The battleship … ?"

"Retribution," said DeTunne.

"More like anger," added Stone.

"The interesting thing," I added, "is that they didn't hit this camp. That means they want someone alive; you, Muna."

She nodded, uncertainly.

"I can see why," I continued. "You're now the figure-head for the Rebels on Earth. They probably want to do a deal with you. They would love a client Queen, or Princess, for a while. Does anybody here have a telescope Muna?"

"Er … I'm not sure. Why?"

"Well, I would like to get a good look at this Ischian battleship…"

"I'll see what I can do."

"I'm going to find myself some hooch, and then get my head down," said DeTunne.

"I wouldn't mind that too," I added. "Later."

"You can use my tent, if it's still standing," Stone offered. "Come on dad,"

Anywhere would do. Stone started to walk and I followed, but there seemed no purpose to our meandering. I felt that he wanted to talk to me about something. "Well, this is a strange mess we find ourselves in Stone."

"Yeah. You can say that again!"

"So wha-..."

"Listen Dad. I was wondering what you've heard from Dee. Actually, I'm itching to know. Is he alright?"

"Well, yeah. Actually he's more than alright. Haven't you heard? He's been working on this tempometer of his. Says it's a form of time travel."

"Yeah, I know. But Dee … ."

"Well, as you know, he has found that wife of yours – what's her name?"

"Shihu. Yes I know about that. It's incredible that he even found her, let alone *alive*! Apparently she dropped into the sea off the coast. Lucky she can swim!"

"You sound so flippant!"

"No Dad. I mean, well of course I am delighted. But *that* relationship was over a long time ago."

"Sorry. So how did he actually find her?"

"An anomaly … . On his temposcope. Obvious really. When is he coming back?"

"Well, he'd be crazy to come back now, *wouldn't he*? I mean. He's in the quietest, safest place in the Solar System... perhaps in the Universe; Earth 30,000 years ago!"

Stone laughed. "Yeah! And tell me again, why didn't this Ambi whassisname communicate with me?"

"I *didn't* say, actually."

"Well?"

"Well, I'm not sure it's that easy to explain. Until you have..."

"Dad?"

"Ha! Well, how can I say this..? I think Kek told me he thinks you are too stubborn... something like that."

"Dad?"

"Well, that's all I can remember."

"Hm… Okay, I'll get the truth out of you later. Let's get back to my tent."

A man stepped out from the gloom of the night. "Are you Jake Nanden?"

"Yes."

"I've been looking for you everywhere! I understand you want a telescope. We have something... It's not SETI 15, but it's something." Both Stone and I looked at each other, confused. We followed him.

Aimed somewhere near where the beams had originated, a strange, long, wooden box stood, supported on a sturdy M49 missile tripod.

"Take a look. I guessed that's what you want to look at."

I stooped to look through the tiny eyepiece. "Wow!" The spaceship I saw looked well beyond any current earth technology. I could hardly pull my eyes away.

"Let me look!" asked Stone. He tapped my shoulder insistently so I stepped away.

"Hm," He said. It's not what I had been expecting. "But … I think I know this ship. I can't be sure..."

"You *know* it?" I exclaimed.

"Yeah. You know that battleship I told you about which had tried to stop us getting back through the worm-hole?"

"Yes … ?"

"Well it looks the same. I think it had the same marking on the side. I can't be sure..."

"Interesting. So tell me again; I forgot what you said about its capabilities?"

"Well apart from being fucki-… sorry, huge, it has some nasty disrupter antennas, or at least one. Oh, and it's piloted by a female. Bitch."

"Hm. Muna could be interested in that. Speaking of which, we should let her see this."

"I'll fetch her," the telescope man said.

While we waited, I asked Stone some things that had been on my mind.

"What was the last thing you heard from Katie?"

"Nothing since the first news of the attack. I tried ordering a vid-link but she never responded … I don't *know* dad."

"And Jay? How … is she?"

"Oh you know … . She wanted me to get a settled job. Not marriage, but you know, something settled. Kids. I guess that's what she's thinking about."

"And..."

"Well … . It's not for me. At least not yet. We argued. Actually, we weren't talking when all *this* happened!" Stone threw up his hands.

Muna arrived and looked through the telescope. "Wow! Shit!"

"You ain't gonna beat that with anything we have on earth," I commented, wryly. "That's what I meant when I said we had to think about taking one."

"So what *is* your plan Jake?" Muna asked.

"Well, the only thing that keeps running through my mind is J5. Two years ago, when he first came back through a wormhole, Stone told me this invasion would happen. I tried to tell some powerful people I know but none except Adam – sorry, the son of a friend of mine – would listen; vested interests, I guess. I put a weapons store in the only safe place I could think of; my mother's back garden on J5. I also buried a powerful radio transmitter with Morse code manuals, which I had distributed to Adam and a number of useful people I know, including some in the Interplanetary Police Patrol service. I don't know who's still alive but they will all be useful. I have to get to J5, first for the weapons. But it might have other uses."

Muna nodded. "And your friend … Adam?"

"I haven't been able to contact him, he's in LA, but you can guarantee he will have some substantial resistance organized!" I didn't tell Muna or stone that Adam and I had planned the resistance in some detail, as a contingency, when Stone had first warned me. I also didn't tell them that Adam, being Gary Enquine's son, would probably have credibility problems, even now. "We need a rallying point," I continued. "Something we can defend, if only against their lighter cruisers. We need a command centre. I know J5 is at least badly damaged but it's the nearest of the J stations and maybe something can be salvaged."

Jake looked sceptically at me and then his feet. I think he knew that I wanted to go to J5 to see if Mary, my mother, still lived.

"*What*?" asked Muna, looking from Stone to me.

I coughed. "A rallying point is not the only way to use J5. Another point is that we don't have anything the size and power of... that *thing*, up there! I did a lot of research before *all this* happened and I know things about J5 that not many know. With enough cruisers, we might make it defensible and give it enough firepower to do some damage... If we can rig some kind of missile launching system..."

"That's if there enough cruisers *left*. Let alone *missiles*!" Stone interjected. "Seems to me guerrilla warfare is a better option against these muthers..."

"Well yeah. For a while... But eventually, if we are to actually beat them, and not simply look forward to years, perhaps centuries, of wearing them down, we need a command centre. Anyway there *is* one other reason … . We may need a distraction at some point … something to pull that ship away from Earth. Any cruiser simply won't do it."

"Like a decoy, you mean?" said Stone.

"Yeah … . You could call it that."

"Shit. Feel sorry for the fuckers who'll be on *that*! Count me out!"

"Stone, your language and anti-bravado must be something in your blood. Katie would be *proud* of you! It's good to hear you back to your old self … . It's been a long time!"

After a pause, Muna spoke. "Well, tomorrow I will show you what's left of the SU 401."

"Oh, one other thing Muna. Stone says he knows this ship. He encountered it though a wormhole. I don't know if you … ."

"I told her, dad."

"Oh. Well tell us again what you know of the captain. It might be useful."

"Hm. Well you'd be better off reading my original report, if you could find it. My recollections were clearer then. Her name's An-shabakthi, or something like that, and her ship is the Lukshitha. What can I say about her? Plenty of gold jewellery. Arrogant, vain...but not too bright. At least not at outwitting humans. I guess she is good enough with her own kind."

Muna replied, "Hm! A bitch, eh? Well she has met her match in *me*!"

***

5 weeks until Zero Hour

"What I want to know is, how did it even get here?" I said, looking at the wrecked space-fighter. "Surely SU 401s were specifically designed for the Mars atmosphere. It can't possibly manage Earth's thick atmosphere."

I looked at the battered SU 401 with some awe. It still looked a beautiful machine. Muna's engineer wiped his hands with an oily rag and grinned:

"Well, it's not common knowledge," he began, "but an SU *can* be landed in Earth's atmosphere. A few tried it in the early days; emergencies during skirmishes with the USAC patrols around the Moon. Dunno if you can take off though, or escape Earth. We *think* it's possible with strengthened wing-lets and the engine on full boost. Just have to try. In any case, I have these babies!" He pulled back a tarpaulin that had been covering some long thin structures, next to the SU. I saw four gleaming ES4800 engines, each one rated twice the power of the old SU units.

"But can you get them mounted on the SU?"

"Ah. Well we can try, can't we?"

I liked the man's attitude.

"Let's have a beer on it... what's your name?" I asked I looked at the oily, boiler-suited man with hair, too oily to guess at the colour, under an oily blue engineer's cap.

"Duffy," he offered. "Just call me Duffy. Though most around here call me Scruff Duffy or just Scruff! Sure. Got a crate right here."

Stone shook his head.

"What's wrong?" I asked him.

"Not the beer. Just the whole thing of you flying … that! I mean you aren't even licensed to that level!"

"Hey nobody said anything about *you* flying this!" commented Duffy "And just *what* level are you licensed to?"

"Civilian. Level three. I only learned to fly since quitting the USAC. I was a good soldier but I never flew one of these!"

Duffy blew a long blast of air through his mouth:

"Well you got a steep learning curve mister. I think I need something stiffer than a beer!"

He pulled open a flap on the side of the SU's sleek fuselage and lifted out a dirty bottle of Johnny Walker, its neck covered by a dirty glass. While we sipped the strong liquor, Duffy walked us over the craft. Long and pencil shaped, with its four PODs arranged around the rear of the fuselage, on the end of long wing-lets, it looked a wonderfully elegant site in the harsh desert; a reminder of the great technological epoch of the USAC and her enemies.

***

4 weeks until Zero Hour

Major Luxmi Davidos regained consciousness but had to control a rising fear when she found she couldn't move. Face down, deep in the air-conditioning bowels of USAC Station 4, commonly referred to as S.4, she had been hiding from the Ischian dogs for nearly fourte hours. She had no idea if any other crew members had survived or not. She shook with the cold.

Remembering her training, she tried to think of something from her childhood to calm herself. She remembered her step-brother, Steve, pushing her on the village swing, higher and higher, until it had gone over the bar and come down behind the giggling Steve, who ended up sprawled on the ground. This moment had inspired her to volunteer for the USAC Air Force. She hadn't passed the fitness test and ended in USAC Ground Forces instead. And now she had ended up here; possibly the last Earth woman, albeit replicant, left alive in the Solar System.

The last order issued by the station Commander had been desperate and simple: disperse to sniper positions and survive until possible reinforcements from S.5 arrived.

"That's a laugh!" she murmured to herself. "Sniper position! Couldn't snipe on a mouse from here!"

When the Ischians had come, they had done so in force and she had to find a bolt-hole. Pushing a panel out of a ceiling in the last empty cabin of a corridor, she had scrambled up into the air-con ducting and escaped her pursuers. The ship had been so badly damaged that the ducting had become twisted in many places, blocked in others. She only just heard a loud bang before something fell on her and she passed out.

Now, she carefully shifted her weight from side to side and found that she could move her legs and arms slightly. She wiggled her fingers and toes. They all seemed intact.

Thank god I'm lying, face down! No damage to that! If I can just get a little way off the floor, I might just lever this thing up, whatever it is. There's my X.259. Good!

Dragging her trusted laser towards her by the butt, she slid it between the heavy object and the floor, right next to her left hip. Squirming from side to side, she found she had enough movement to get her elbows underneath her and push. She pushed with her knees too, until she reached a kneeling position. The weight of the seribdenum girder, for she could see now that it *was* a girder, bore down terribly on her back. She could feel blood trickling from the skin over her spine, soaking into her combat jacket and T-shirt. Sweating and gasping, she continued to push, until finally she achieved a foetal position, with all the weight balanced on her back and knees. Her arms were free. She propped up the beam with the laser, stood on end, and then relaxed.

For a few minutes, she lay there gasping. When she had recovered, she crawled a little further down the duct. She found what she had been looking for; a filter casing, bent, but strong enough. She dragged it back to the girder and wedged it underneath. Using her back as the lever, she forced the girder up one last time and removed her laser before letting the beam's weight settle on the filter casing.

Now all I have to do is worry about food and water! They have no way of knowing I'm here.

One of only five officers left alive on the flight deck when the last command had been issued, she had decided to switch off the Internal Detection filters for the station; S.4 had been overrun anyway and if the aliens did figure out how to operate the equipment quickly, they could use this to locate any surviving personnel. It had been her last duty as Station Facilities Engineer. Now she was just another USAC grunt but a survivor. She had to go *on surviving* until the relief from S.5 arrived, if it ever did.

***

3 weeks until Zero Hour

I heard the four ES4800 engines burst into life. Sitting back in the G-seat, I tightened the harness one last notch before signalling to Duffy to release the restraining bolts on the makeshift launch-pad.

I glanced at Stone, who forced a smile through clenched teeth. Then I took a deep breath and pushed the boost control to two-thirds. The SU 401, now rebuilt and heavily modified, shook heavily on the pad. My teeth rattled in my head.

It's quite possible this is going to shake itself to death!

I gritted my teeth and stared at the utter blue sky above. Slowly, almost imperceptibly at first, the rusty horizon of the Utah desert slipped below the rear edge of the cockpit as the old spacecraft tottered and lurched upwards. I had a hard time controlling the pitch and yaw using the sensitive controls. The sophistication of the craft felt way beyond anything I had experienced before; Stone had been right!

Suddenly, one of the huge engines cut out. I knew this because a whole bank of red lights flared up on the dashboard, and the ship seemed to go into a corkscrew, with the auto-gyros struggling to to regain control. The corkscrew became more violent and out of control. With my pulse going through the roof, I pressed the manual control button and used the joy-stick to try countering the violent motion. At first, my attempts were clumsy and made things worse.

"Come on! You miserable son of a bitch!"

Finally, when I had almost given up and the ground loomed, barely 100 feet below, I felt the first easing of the violent motion and knew that I was regaining control. The corkscrew eased and the little ship levelled out into a smooth, straight path. With one engine out, the motion of the aircraft felt skewed. I tried to compensate using the trim tabs on the wing-lets and let the autopilot take over.

It came as a great relief when the first dash of stratus cloud appeared; I was leaving Earth's atmosphere. At any moment, I had expected either to fall to Earth in a blazing heap of seribdenum or to be blasted out of the sky by an Ischian cruiser.

Neither happened and, with intense satisfaction, I found myself pointing the nose of the SU 401 into the infinite blackness of space, towards the blip of J5 indicated on my pre-programmed nav panel.

I pressed the button for a beer on the tiny n-gen in the cockpit; a gift from Muna.

***

3 weeks until Zero Hour
The ship's navigation officer on duty aboard the Lukshîa still felt hung-over from the previous 'night's revelries. He didn't notice the small blip leaving Earth on his radar monitor. He carried on sleeping. None of the other cruisers in the area of space over Utah had any reason to suspect an Earth-made vessel still existed so they didn't bother to contact the blip on their screens for identification.

***

3 weeks until Zero Hour
It felt good to be back in space. As I left Earth, for a while I had nothing better to do than muse over the previous night's conversations.

It had taken almost ten days to repair the SU, with all Duffy's men, and many others, co-opted. We worked flat out, day and night. Finally, we were almost ready for launch. It only remained for Muna, her cohorts, Stone and I to discuss our tactics. DeTunne had come along for the ride. He wallowed in a mire of whiskey-fuelled thoughts, to one side of the tent.

"We need a plan," I said.

Muna continued to sip a glass of wine for some time, before saying, "I don't have one."

I took a deep breath. "Look, Muna. It's clear these aliens want you alive. That's a big advantage to us, but it also indicates they consider you the biggest risk. You

have now defeated the Ischians in battle! With that reputation, and the myth that surrounds you, I think you're the
ideal focus point for any forces left able to fight on Earth.
Also, the experience gained from defeating them will be
very useful. I think you should unite the forces on Earth
and lead an attack at a designated time, to be relayed to
you, once the forces off-Earth are prepared, whatever they
are."

"Why me? I mean, I know the reasons you have mentioned. You probably don't know this but we have just
heard that in Los Angeles, the resistance are preparing to
launch an attack on the Ischians..."

I sat bolt upright. "Who? You mean Gary Enquine?"

Muna looked surprised. "No! Possibly his son might
be involved. It's rumoured … ."

"Mm. It could be a trick by the Ischians." I didn't believe but I didn't to field any awkward questions.

"Maybe," Muna continued. "But they are asking for us
to launch an attack on Washington at the same time, perhaps in the next month,"

"Perhaps. Maybe, yes if we're ready. But we have to
find out if it's genuine. We need somebody to get in there
and find out. Like Washington, there is probably a way
in. … ."

"I could send a man?" she replied.

"I want to go," Stone said, suddenly.

"No … I wouldn't be happy with that," I replied. I
faced Muna. "I want Stone to say with you, and DeTunne
too. Both could be very useful."

"Of course. Stone will be one of my Lieutenants; after
his last performance, it seems only fair. A resourceful
man … . As for your friend … ."

She cast a glance at the drunk DeTunne. He glared at
us, hearing his name mentioned.

"You'd be surprised," I countered. "He's a very good
soldier. He will sober up, if there's something useful for

him to do. We need somebody we really trust to go to Los Angeles.”

But Stone had already got to his feet and announced:

“But I *want* to go. I *have* to go!” he declared.

“Why?” I demanded.

“Because I can be *useful*. I’m resourceful! I proved that through the wormhole, and in the battle today.” He clenched his fists stubbornly. I knew I wouldn’t dissuade him. Fighting Stone is just inviting him to do what he wants behind your back. I held up my hands and looked to Muna for support.

“It’s my decision,” she objected. “You’re my Lieutenant now Stone. If you want to take complete responsibility for this resistance, Jake Nanden, then fine, you make the decision. Otherwise, it’s up to me.”

I shrugged. I had been outmanoeuvred by both of them.

“What’s wrong Muna?” Stone said, looking at the Princess. She held her head in her hands.

“I don’t know. I have been suffering really bad headaches since the battle. Probably the noise. Maybe a bit of concussion. It’s nothing. Or maybe the heat. It never did agree with me.”

“And you’re living in the desert!” quipped Stone. She grinned.

I drew a long breath and looked at my son. He grinned at me.

I announced, “Time for me to get some sleep.”

***

3 weeks until Zero Hour

I was approaching J5. I could see it, hanging in space like a giant, metallic ring-doughnut, made or silver and glass and more than 5 miles in diameter. It had housed more than 100,000 people. But no longer did it sparkle with fairy lights. No longer did it spin. It appeared to be dead. My ship’s computer had calculated the approach and it looked like it would intersect correctly with J5's docking station. This would leave me with the fairly simple task, even for a low-grade space pilot like myself, of using the thrusters to execute the final docking. Even if J5's power supply had been knocked out, the simple mechanical bolts that would hold the SU's docking hatch to the great space station would still operate, provided they had been left in the open position. I felt confident and my old home seemed to approach me out of the gloom like a welcoming parent. Only its outer rim showed, highlighted by the light of the sun. The rest could only be distinguished by total blackness, a lack of stars.

On my screen, the computer displayed a wireframe of the great station, showing that my course still looked correct for the docking point.

But when only a kilometre from the docking bay, I saw that I would miss it by more than the thrusters could compensate for, on the tiny amount of hydrogen left in the tanks.

How can this happen?

I could only speculate briefly that the J Station must be on an erratic course, perhaps caused by damaged to its structure. I had no more time to think about it.

I pressed the ignition switch for the three remaining big engines but nothing happened!

Somewhere, something on the propulsion system had failed, which I shouldn't have surprised me. I felt lucky to have made it off Earth.

There seemed only one thing to do. Closing my helmet and switching the suit-oxygen supply on, I opened the EVA locker. In a new craft, there would be a small, waist-mountable thruster kit as well as the safety cord. As I had expected, the thruster kit had gone but the cord still lay there. I coiled it hastily and clipped one end to my belt. Punching the canopy emergency release switch, I released my safety harness. As soon as the cockpit had decompressed, the canopy ejected and drifted away from the craft.

The SU-401 had been designed as a two-man ship. I struggled to turn around in my seat and reached through to the EVA locker in the weapons officer compartment. I just managed to grab the second safety cord as it floated out. I clipped the end to the free end of my cord. Now I would have twice the distance to travel before I would have to abandon the SU. Standing up on the seat, I aimed my head towards the docking bay of the J Station, allowed for deflection and pushed off as hard as I could. I had just enough time to think how unlikely this manoeuvre would be to succeed before a change in my orientation warned me to pay attention to the cord. I tried to spool it out from my hands evenly but my body continued twisting. Soon, I found myself facing the SU-401, which sailing serenely on into empty space. I could hear my own heavy breaths. Sweat formed on my brow and remained there because of the zero-gravity. I stretched my neck to see where I my trajectory would take me. To my intense relief, it looked like I would impact the docking hub, somewhere. It only remained to be seen if this would happen before the cord ran out. Looking down at the coil, I could only see about ten coils left; about twenty feet. I prepared to unhook the cord end from my waist clip. I had come *so* close to the hub now!

Damn!

Almost within arm's length of the Station skin, I had to unclip. My head banged into seribdenum and I twisted around to find a handhold. Just above me, I saw some kind of ducting bracket. I squirmed around and grabbed it.

Safe!

Gasping for breath, I twisted around to watch for one last moment before the SU-401 disappeared from view, behind the hub rim. Now, I had no way off of the station, unless one of its survival POD's remained intact.

Unlikely.

I reached around and grabbed the bracket with the other hand. Hauling myself along the surface of the station, I slowly worked my way towards a protuberance which I soon identified as a docking ring. In it, or nearby, would be an emergency hatch. Sure enough, I could see the tell-tale red release handle In the middle of the ring. If J5's power had been completely knocked out, I would have to turn it manually; something I had never tried. At least I wouldn't have to worry about an access code. Gripping the handle, I pressed the release with my thumb and twisted the handle with my wrist.

Doesn't move!

I held it awkwardly with both gloved hands and wrenched it with such force that I span around the docking ring, only just managing to hold on to it with one hand.

Damn! Got to do this!

Returning to a position with both hands on the handle, I found something to brace my feet against and applied a steady force. At the end of my exertion, the handle budged slightly. I tried again and it moved a bit more, then a bit more, until I had it turned through one hundred and eighty degrees. I saw a puff of dust as some remaining compressed air escaped from the pneumatic locking system. The four bolts in the inner face of the annular ring released and the whole port opened an inch. I didn't see any sign of air escaping, which meant no atmospheric pressure remained inside. It confirmed that the station was completely dead.

I pushed the port. It slowly swung inwards. I pushed myself through the opening and closed the port halfway behind me. The sun's rays provided just enough light to see. A long tunnel stretched out before me. I felt like I had entered a vast tomb. Long rows of seats, for arriving crews during re-pressurisation, lined both sides of the tunnels. Next to each, a com unit had been placed. I couldn't resist trying one but of course it proved to be dead. I felt like the loneliest man in the Universe

Solitude has a curious way of calming one. I glided to the bulkhead at the end of the compartment. I could see a control panel above a small door with a porthole but I could see no light through the porthole. The procedure for opening the inner hatch would be the same as for the outer. But when I tried to twist the handle, it wouldn't budge. I tried several more times, even bracing my feet on a sill, before halting.

Seems to be jammed. I have to think.

I remembered something about some auxiliary docking ports having their hatches wired to permanent lock by default when the power had been cut. This had been during the first scare about alien invasion when I served on Io. Being a nerd, growing up on J5, I had subscribed to the Station's maintenance journal, J-Tech-5.

I remember reading the article:

> Emergency battery supply to six of the 48 Auxiliary Docking Ports to be disconnected, which will mean, in the case of power cut, the spring-loaded locking bolts will remain engaged, thus confusing, and disrupting an invading enemy.

Perhaps this is one of those ports. But I can't remember the numbers!

I looked at the control panel for the port. I saw the number AP-26 – Auxiliary Port 26.

No. I can't remember if this is one of those or not! Maybe it's something else. Maybe there is still some juice in the emergency battery for one of these locks. If it's the outer one; this one…

I opened the access panel for the door controls. A bunch of wires met my gaze in the dim light. Tracing each wire, I found the one I wanted. Taking the MonRussian knife from the belt on the SU's suit, I cut the wire.

I tried the handle again. This time, it slowly turned.

Yes!

I thought of the god, Mech.

This time, Mech has come through for me! Ha! And I'm not even a replicant.

I had no idea why the power was still flowing only to the outer relay but if it had been to both, I would have not been able to get in. Opening the hatch, I returned to the outer hatch and sealed it. I passed through the inner hatch and sealed that.

I'm in!

Gliding through long corridors, which were cluttered with floating debris, I made my way to the main control deck. In almost every corridor, I saw evidence of fighting: limbs, torn from their bodies, floating past me; blood on the walls; laser holes in walls and control boxes.

It's a mess!

At last, I reached the hatch to the control deck. It had been sealed shut. But with no power, it could be opened easily enough. I braced myself and twisted the large handle. It didn't move. I exerted my full strength and the handle finally turned. Suddenly, it jerked free, making me lose my foothold. I swung around the port and came to rest, facing away from the port. I remained still for a moment to regain by breath.

Something touched my shoulder. Shock made me pull away from the touch. I gasped, turned and saw an unsuited body float past me, silently, eerily, like a spirit leaving a body.

As a soldier, I had become used to seeing dead bodies. Seeing a dead man on J5 seemed different; it was my home. In space, if cold enough, bodies freeze and don't decay. I could see this one had partly decayed.

There must have been some warmth for a time after this man died.

I passed through the hatch into the main Control Room. Confronting me were long rows of dead control panels and display screens. To the right, I saw a large transparent seribdenum window, largely broken, which looked out across the vast inner space of J5. What I could see through it horrified me. The vast, inner space of J5 had become congested with a myriad of the objects of everyday life; bits of houses, tractors, dead cows, human bodies, garbage, hover-cars, hoverbikes and strangest of all, dead birds. All floated like so much jetsom in the great torus.

I had to brace myself for a moment. The thought, faint but insistent in the back of my mind for so long, that my mother, Mary, might still be alive, could no longer be sustained. If there had been any human, or even alien, life left on J5, it would have cleared up this mess. Unless she escaped somehow, my mother had to be dead. The enormity of the feeling rendered me motionless for that longest moment of my life.

Finally, I came to my senses. I had thirty minutes of oxygen left. To stay alive, I had to first find an air supply, then water and lastly, food.

I headed for the maintenance depot. As I approached the oxygen store room, I expected to find its door locked. It had been smashed open. Clearly, the last survivors had been here before me. With the main station structure compromised, there would have been no other source of oxygen, apart from the survival PODs. There were several large, industrial size tanks left but these would be too big for me to use. I counted forty-eight full tanks left on the racks. Each one would last at least 10 hours, so I had 20 days' worth of oxygen. I pulled two tanks off the rack and made for the nearest emergency exit.

Now, my problem would be finding an intact survival POD. This would be my best chance of finding, not only food and water supplies, but also an atmosphere in which to consume them. There had been 100,000 inhabitants on J5, with 1000 survival PODs to serve them. These were placed mostly around the rim of the five-mile diameter torus. It might take me days to find an intact one if most of the inhabitants had escaped. Sure enough, the first POD docking bay proved empty. I tried three more before having to change my oxygen tank. I began to feel very tired now. I faced a choice; sleep in the suit or make further attempts to find a POD.

The image of the large oxygen tanks kept passing through my mind. Suddenly I knew why. They were usually used for the maintenance POD; a small POD that could travel around the exterior of J5, carrying staff to locations for repair. The tanks were for its limited internal atmosphere.

If it's still here...

I made my way wearily back to the maintenance depot.

There should be a long corridor here, leading to the skin … . There it is!

I hauled myself along it, noting little sign of damage. I reached the end and located the POD hatch. Peering through the window, I could see the POD. Now I just needed its batteries to be intact. I opened the hatch and climbed into the POD. Sealing the hatch, I pressed the systems start switch. To my surprise, the dash lights all came on. Their flashing and sparkling looked like a Christmas tree, at least to me!

Disengaging the docking clamps, I eased the small craft out of the bay and started towards the torus rim. I kept a sharp eye out for any lights; a sign of life.

At a speed of about six miles per hour, the little POD took me around the rim of the station. I passed many empty POD bays. This heartened me because it meant there could be many survivors but I had nearly given up hope of finding one intact when I saw it. POD 335 remained in its bay. I went in for a closer look. It looked undamaged.

Probably faulty release mechanism.

I returned to the maintenance bay. Looking more closely at the torus of J5, I could see that many of the outer transparent panels were broken. Each one not only admitted light but generated electricity for the station. Indeed, these panels were one of the main source of power and would have to be fixed simply to get the torus turning once more.

But that's for tomorrow!

It took another hour to reach POD 335 in my suit. As I had hoped, it remained completely intact. Once I had climbed inside it, I pressurised the POD. Intense relief swept over me when I could finally take the suit off. I even took a shower. Then I broke open the provisions; enough on board to keep one hundred people alive for a week. For me, it would be enough for two years!

Tomorrow, I will start to repair the outer skin of the Station; a very laborious process.

Settling down on one of the comfortable bunks, I slept for nearly 18 hours.

***

3 weeks until Zero Hour

I awoke with my mind fully engaged. I had that familiar feeling that somebody had been talking to me.

"Kek-suîxjh? Is that you?"

"Hello fellow traveller. Yes. I have been catching up with the news. You are surprisingly talkative when you are only half-awake!"

"Shame on you Kek-suîxjh. That's not fair! I might have told you anything!"

"Might? You already have!"

"Ha! Where are you now?"

"Within one of your Earth days from the anomaly. I am looking forward to this. The Pet Sounds is a fine ship but even I get lonely out here..."

"Well, I wanted to talk to you anyway. I have escaped from Earth and I'm now on one of our great space stations, the one I grew up on, in fact."

"Yes, I know."

"Now, I guess I have to start thinking about organising some resistance. I need to generate... create... I don't know the right phrase... I need to pull people together so I guess I need some kind of feeling of community. This has never been my strong point; feeling part of a community, I mean. Let alone creating one. For me, I think it would mean putting the Blue Path, and the Paths of the Universal-mind on the back burner for a while..."

"Back burner?"

"Um. Make them a lower priority .... I need solitude for those. It was the life I had chosen..."

"You sound sad. Sometimes you have to set apart the quest for God; when your community needs you, for an instance. Without your community, there is nobody to worship your god. Some would say; without community, there can be no god. I am sure you will be fine Jake."

Kek-suîxjh pronounced my name with a guttural, soft 'J'. He always managed to make it sound like a term of affection.

"To be honest, it's not such a sacrifice. Since the loss of Katie and my child, Daniel, I have struggled with my faith. Well, I guess I better get up. I have a gigantic task ahead of me; getting this station up and running again. One last thing Kek-suîxjh. Those battleships that the Ischian Imperial Fleet are using; I need to know as much as possible about them. We aim to take one. Could you ask Ambi-xjhu about them?"

"I certainly will. As soon as possible. Good bye young Jake."

"Good bye Kek-suîxjh."

I went through some morning exercises but felt distracted. I fixed myself a strong coffee in the POD's n-gen and sat down.

Abandoning the Blue Path, or even just putting it on a hold, while I became involved in military matters, did not appeal to me. I wasn't the same man I had been, or the replicant I thought I had been, when still in the USAC Army.

After leaving the Army, I bummed around a while, looking for a cause I could stick to, but the voice in my head, which turned out to be Kek-suîxjh, convinced me that I was worthy of spiritual growth. I read widely and listened to many speakers on beliefs as diverse as Buddhism, Judaism, Islam and even Mech. Then I heard of Arial Jefferies.

Nicknamed 'The Pastor,' Jefferies proved a hard man to pin down, both spiritually and physically. I finally managed to track him down on Mars. The advert said he would be giving a private talk to inmates of a prison-mine but I managed to bribe my way in.

"The Blue Patt … ." he began, "… is *not* a religion, it's a belief." He stared at the confused faces and then smiled. "There *is* no *God* in this belief. It is a path, a path to enlightenment, or if you like, wisdom. Yes, it teaches abstinence, modesty, courtesy, inner peace but most of all it teaches communication. We think about, not only what is the price of solitude, but what is the reward of solitude."

Jefferies paused before continuing:

"Let's just wait while that sinks in. If that resonates with you, then the Blue Path is for you. If not, then there are free drinks and sandwiches at the back; see you later! You see, solitude is the aim, solitude the ideal. For those of you that will join me, solitude is what you have strived for all your life. Without knowing it. Oh yes, you will have thought you were lonely. You will have struggled against it but, deep down, you knew it was what you wanted, the way *forward*!"

I felt jolted by what he said, because I agreed with him.

He continued, "And the reason it's the way forward is because we cannot ever, really communicate unless we are… isolated, independent; shorn of the emotional burden of those around us. And indeed, shorn of our own emotional burden. There are many forms of intelligence out there. I am not just talking about communicating with humans, or even other animals on Earth. That has been done. I am talking about the next stage of man's development; reaching out to the stars."

A lot of us, myself included, were nodding.

He went on, "Now, I am gonna say something controversial. Some of us have *heard* from being in outer space already. Yes, you know what I'm talking about. I'm quite sure at least three of you in the audience have heard a voice in your head. For some of you, this may go back a few years, some perhaps up to ten years. Those, my friends, are aliens; Ischians. And perhaps even some other species, who knows? Now, in a minute I am going to open this up so that you can ask me questions. Then I am going to give any of you who want one my book."

I didn't ask any questions but I hung around until I could get close enough to talk to him.

"You one of the guards? Some kind of undercover cop?" he asked me.

I laughed uncomfortably. "No."

"I ask 'cause you look a bit too cool for a convict." He peered more closely at my face. "Wait! Don't I know you from somewhere?"

"You might do. But that doesn't matter. I am very interested in this Blue Path. I want to know more."

"Good. Here! Take a book. Read it an-…"

"No. What I mean is that I have heard those voices … well, one."

"Um hm…"

"For about twenty-seven years. It's hard to say precisely how long…"

"Ah hah … . Listen Mister. Even I have only been hearing them for just under twenty years! Wait, I do know you. You're that Nanden guy, aren't you? The space pilot or some such … ."

"Yeah. Army."

"Sure. I remember. Anyway, I get loads of cranks so stop winding me up. I'm a busy man these days."

"No. I'm serious. I really have heard this voice for nearly twenty-seven years."

That's how I came to know Arial Jefferies personally. I managed to convince him that I told him the truth and we communicated using coms for a few months. Then I went to a few more of his talks and joined the Blue Path. I would soon come to call him a good friend.

The Blue Path made sense of everything to me; my intense loneliness, my frequent need for solitude, and the voice of Kek-suîxjh. This belief had something had to offer both species. It could draw us together. *That* did seem something worth fighting for. I began to think of the Blue Path as the *human* end of the inter-species vidphone.

Sitting in my POD on J5, I wondered if Jefferies had survived. It occurred to me for the first time that I might be the only Blue Path adherent left alive. As well as taking my wife, mother and second son, now it looked as if the Imperial Ischians might deflect me from my belief, at least for a while. But I had to survive and help others to fight back, if only so that I could find Stone again. If he was dead, and yes, I had to come to terms with the possibility, then I had to do it for the rest of mankind. It was with a heavy heart that I went to work.

***

2 weeks until Zero Hour

"It's incredible. I can't believe it's just sitting there. I mean... just look at it!" Stone peered over the shallow dirt ridge at the ticking-hot freight train, static on the track in the dry desert. Its rusting wheels had not moved for almost twenty years, watched over by look-outs from three different tribes whose intersecting borders it straddled. Stone turned to the guard who had led them to the ridge.

"And you say the other tribes have agreed to let us just walk in and take it?" he continued.

Nodding, still with his binocular clip-ons, the man remained silent.

Stone glared at the train. Through a heat-haze that made the far end of the train quiver like a mirage, Stone could see several Amtrak logos on wagon-sides. Of all the rusting miles of paint, they alone stubbornly declared the name of a company long since vanished. Stone fidgeted and opened his mouth.

"Looks clear," the guard said wryly.

"Well … is *it*?"

"Guess there's only one way to find out Gov." The use of the abbreviated 'Gov' sounded like an insult. Stone Ignored it.

"Yeah. Let's go." Stone reached out behind him and beckoned for the other eleven men, including the drunk DeTunne, forward. When they arrived, he stood up. The guard hesitated and then stood up beside Stone. "Follow me," Stone said, quietly. "Nobody do anything sudden, and stay close the train, once we get there."

Crossing the hundred yards or so to the nearest freight-wagon was one of the scariest moments of Stone's life.

"Tell me again the inventory for the train. What's in these wagons?" he said to the guard, swallowing. His voice cut across the hot, dry sound of crickets and cracking scrub like a knife.

"Livestock – now dead – refrigerators, auto-parts, electronics, agricultural equipment, *munitions*."

They reached the edge of the track and twenty-four boots crunched on the gravel ballast.

"Munitions. I like the sound of that. Near the front, right?" The guard didn't answer. "This is the most dangerous part." Stone picked out the two rearmost men. "You two, cut loose the rear four carriages. The rest of you, deploy to defensive positions, on top and at the base of the waggons. Nice and easy."

When the four cattle-waggons had been decoupled, they continued towards the front of the train. It stretched almost a mile long. As they went, they checked each set of wheels and couplings for obstructions or damage.

The first thin slice of afternoon shadow provided some relief from the relentless sun. They finally reached the faded yellow diesel engine at the front of the long train. The guard with Stone signalled to other guards, stationed on a shallow bluff a hundred yards to the right of the track.

"All clear," he said, reading their signal reply.

"Okay. Duff," said Stone. "Let's get in the cab; see what state it's in."

Stone followed the mechanic up the short ladder to the cab. The driver's door had been left open. Its hinges were rusty and squeaked as Stone brushed past it. The sound made him grit his teeth.

While Duffy used an old screwdriver to open panels, sometimes forcing them with the flat of the blade when the screws were too rusted, Stone peered through the dirty glass windows to the no-man's land beyond the train.

"It's a mess!" said the engineer. "As I thought, the heat has made junk of most of it." Stone didn't say anything. He knew Duffy was prone to be pessimistic. "Luckily it's a dry heat. Nothing's corroded. Let's give it a go."

Duffy pressed the red ignition switch. Stone heard the sound of straining relays and a cough somewhere. These were followed by a single click and silence. Duffy pressed the switch again but nothing happened. "Fuse has gone. Still some juice in the batteries but not much. I'll need to take a look at the engines. I reckon they have just seized up in the heat."

"How long?"

"…is a piece of string... Tonight, at least!"

Duffy worked through the night, by torchlight. He and Stone kept watch for any attacks from the rival tribes while others rested uneasily, drinking beer.

Stone paced up and down for a while. One of the guards came up to him carrying a can of warm beer.

"Come and sit down mate – rest your legs. There ain't nothin' you can do here. If they do attack, we won't see 'em. Matter of fact; that was somefin' I was gonna ask..."

Stone took the beer gladly and relented, following the guard to the fire.

"What were you going ask?" he said, after draining half a can in one go.

"How did Her Highness swing it? I mean; there has been a guard detail out here for the last two years, watching this old train. There was a truce, sure, but how did she get them to let us just... walk right in … and take it?"

"Well … it took some doin'. But I think basically they just believed her. She told them we needed it to fight the Ischians. She has a lot of credibility after beating the crap out of those aliens."

"After *we* beat the crap outta them!" a voice said in the dark.

"You were there?" Stone asked. "It was a close thing."

"Yep. Sure. But Muna always comes through..."

"The old 'gel." somebody else said, sniggering.

"And I bet your father had something to do with the credibility too..." continued the guard.

Stone coughed. "Maybe … "

"Who's his daddy, then?" said a voice in the dark.

"None other than Jake Nanden," answered the guard.

"Ah! Makes sense," replied the questioner.

"But what I don't understand is what are we gonna do with it?" asked another voice. "I mean... we are taking it west, right? Where to? And why?"

"And what is your *plan*?" asked another voice.

"Yeah... And no... disrespect but you are younger than the rest of us. What gives *you* the authority to lead us? I mean; apart from your father's blood, kid."

"One at a time, please gentlemen," Stone replied. "Hm. I'll answer the last question first, since that's the hardest. You're right; I *am* young but have any of you been through a wormhole? Have any of you fought the alien cruisers in a space-battle? I have. And I led a squad towards the end of the battle the other day. Yes, my surname means something but I think Muna rates me as a grunt for my own … erm … virtues … ." Stone paused. He heard a cough and grunt which sounded like a half-chuckle. Then silence. He could hear only the crackling of the fire and chirping of crickets but he felt he had begun to win them round. "And I could smoke any chumsmoker under the table." A chorus of belly-laughs told him he had won them over.

"Why am I in charge of this mission? Not exactly sure. I have some training as a journalist. That was after I graduated from the Academy as a space-pilot." His audience gave a collective gasp. "Anyway, Muna asked me to do a piece on the battle for the Rebel paper she is printing. Some of you may have seen a copy. We are taking some copies with us to LA; if the aliens are going to block radio and laser communications, we'll have to use the printing press!"

The men chuckled.

"Anyway, the point is that Muna is offering the contents of this train as a good-will gesture to the LA Rebels. That's how she persuaded these other groups, or tribes as you call them, to let it go. She wants me to be some kind of Robin Hood. Ha! Ha!" Silences met his laugh. "In her name, of course," Still he heard only silence. "Robin Hood? You've heard of him?"

"I ain't!" said DeTunne, before spitting.

"Ah. Well for those of you not versed in 12th Century history, Robin Hood was a warrior outlaw, like us. He was famous for stealing from the rich to give to the poor."

"Good man," replied the guard. Some of the other voices laughed.

"The aim," Stone continued, "… is to bring all the Rebel groups together, possibly under The Princess. Anyway, I think I'm going to get some sleep. We have a big day tomorrow."

"There's just one other detail," said one of the voices.
"What?"

"There is a section of track blasted away just ahead of the train. That's why it stopped!"

"Yes. In the morning, we are going to shift some rails from behind the train to the front. It will be hard work but it has to be done." He grinned.

"Oh no!" There were collective groans and exclamations of dissatisfaction.

"Get some sleep, until your shift," he added. "As for where we're going. If Duffy can get the diesel started, we are going to try for LA. Nobody knows what the state of track is between here and there. Most likely we will not get that far, and even if we do make it that far, the aliens have one of those domes over the city and they will probably try to stop us..."

"But I heard we cannot get through those domes," commented the guard.

"We only want to deliver the goods to whoever *can* get through the dome. There is... apparently a way in. And the resistance is active inside the dome."

"But I still don't understand *why* we are just giving away all this precious merchandise..?"

Stone kept silent.

Dawn in the desert comes suddenly. The guard woke Stone, who kicked DeTunne, in his sleeping-bag. The old sop groaned and swore. He struggled out of the bag as the rest of the men scratched their crotches and rubbed their heads.

By midday, the two sections of track had been carried to the front of the train and replaced the bent ones that they had removed. The men were exhausted and dehydrated by the time they clambered onto a half empty wagon, just behind the train. Looted and broken refrigerators and cookers lined the side of the track beside it.

"Time to roll!" Stone announced. "Duff, is this gonna work?"

"It should do. It won't pass any inspections but should get us to the West Coast, *if* you can find a way through … ."

Duffy and Stone looked nervously at the red ignition switch. Stone nodded and Duffy pressed it firmly with his oily thumb. They heard the sound of electric motors turning over and a blast of air from the exhaust and then a very loud cough. A thick, black cloud of smoke rose from the engine, up into the still desert air and the engine stopped.

"No problem!" Duffy yelled. "I expected that." He rubbed his hands together, placed his primed thumb over the red button and suddenly pressed it. A deep throbbing sound started a moment later. The engine began to vibrate rhythmically.

"Yes!" shouted Stone.

"Never had a doubt," said Duffy.

"Show me the controls and then go. Muna will be waiting for you."

The train sped over the Utah desert, only slowing down for junctions or to stop while the points were changes, tracks were cleared of derelict trains, or repaired. Always, they headed west, making for Los Angeles. Stone had resolved to get through with their precious cargo. But he had reckoned without the ruthlessness of Commander A-schian'bakî in the space-battleship Lukshîa's, floating ominously above the North Pole.

***

12 days until Zero Hour

Commander of the Ischian Fleet and Commander of Earth, A-schian'bakî, was not in a good mood. She left the bridge and, as she stepped out of the elevator onto the 53rd deck, she kicked a lowly corporal in the hind-legs, sending him sprawling across the biomium floor. She rarely exercised this violence, one of the privileges of her rank. Now she found the sadistic pleasure somewhat made up for the loss in battle of her favourite sexual toy.

Her angry mood made her long, black ears prick. She reached the highly dangerous Main Drive area of the deck and glared furiously at the retina-profile reader, to open the doors. The thick doors 'swished' open and she kicked a guard who had not prostrated himself quickly enough.

"Next time I'll kill you," she barked.

Dressed in an enviro-suit, she entered the most highly-defended area of the ship where the most top secret project had been initiated. All she wanted to do was go to her cabin; an Ischian male waited there patiently to satisfy her. But she had to do something important first.

Securely fixed in the centre of a large chamber criss-crossed with cables, ducts and gangways, lay the mutilated body of the ischian named Chu-anomm. From the stumps of amputated limbs and ducting inserted into her torso and head, ran pipes and electrical cabling. The umbilical tubes and cables connected her to monitors and pumps, placed in a rough rectangle around the harness. Intermittently, a blue glow edged around cabinets and cables, making the air sizzle slightly. It made A-schian'bakî's fur stand on end. She knew she would only safe inside the chamber for a maximum of three hundred and thirty beats. The technicians were all volunteers and would not survive until the end of the mission. The intense radiation from the gravitational distortion, and the constant disruption of their inner organs, could not be countered by any Ischian technology yet.

A-schian'bakî felt sick. She ignored the enviro-suited technicians, who fussed around the body, and spoke into empty space.

"Is the subject ready for Phase Two now?"

One of the technicians walked uncertainly towards the Commander.

"She has made contact with the subject. We are ready to administer the drug-cocktail whenever you wish Commander."

"May I communicate with her?"

"That will not be possible Commander. She is now within the space-time void. Her conscious mind inhabits a continuum beyond our reach..."

"*Yes*! I *know* all that blurb. Only the souls and all that... But can you bring her back briefly?"

The Chief Technician considered this request for a moment. "I would not advise that, Commander. We are at the limit of our technology as it is. We have struggled to get this far…"

"Very well. Inject the drug."

A-schian'bakî spun around and left the chamber.

This would be awkward for her. Chu-anomm came from a poor family. A gifted para-psychic, she had entered into the programme for one reason: to earn financial security for her family. But there had been many conditions. The State had been most emphatic that the mission commander should communicate a final message from her family; 'We love you Chu-anomm. Good luck and sleep with Vîu'

She had been determined to deliver the message, even though it mentioned the outlawed god.

A-schian'bakî had been impatient. Now, she would not be able to communicate this message. Her anger increased. After taking off the suit, she stormed back to her cabin-suite.

She felt only mildly-calmed by the naked Ischian male, lying naked on her bed.

"Make me a drink; Jzu-serinî. It's on the table."

She quickly showered and pulled on a loose robe.

"What was your name again?" she continued. "Doesn't matter. You probably won't live long enough. I'm warning you; I am in a bad mood. If I'm not satisfied with you... Now, I saw you in the main 40th deck canteen, didn't I? I was impressed with the way you walked and … hm … your beautiful, pale ears. I hope you have a large pdudem between your legs. But we'll soon find out."

She lay on the bed and let him lick her all over, starting with her ears. When she felt sufficiently aroused, she pulled off her robe and mounted him. His pdudem looked hard so she lowered herself onto it and pounded him into the pillow. She pounded out all her anger and frustration. She thought, if possible, she should pound him to death. The male felt terrified but tried to smile when possible, ingratiatingly and adoringly. The effort, he reflected ruefully, seemed much harder than the sex.

Finally, his Commander lay exhausted on top of him. A large female, she nearly suffocated him with her weight before she finally declared:

"Go! You'll live! But only just."

She slept and, in her dreams, she saw the Earth warrior princess roasting on an Ischian spit.

***

10 days until Zero Hour

Muna pulled a shawl round her and left her tent in the desert. She couldn't sleep. She had always had bad dreams. She had always had the strange ability to sense the mental state of others, even when they were a million miles away.

"Psychic," the local Mexican preacher had called it,

"Crackpot mumbo-jumbo!" her father had called it, until the night he staggered into her bedroom, woke her up and told her he and her mother had been abducted by aliens just before she had been born.

"Daddy!" she sobbed, scared. She clung to him until he rocked her to sleep. Then he rocked her mother to sleep in the same way.

He never mentioned crackpot mumbo-jumbo again.

This power she had mixed with her dreams. Frequently she could tell apart a dream and 'remote sensing' as some called it.

Her ability marked her as different and set her apart from others. She joined the Rebel Alliance when it still prospered and quickly rose to be a squad leader. When the Alliance began to disintegrate, she became a regional leader. Then came Attica.

Attica prison! The name filled her with dread.

The memory of it made her shudder. She thought she heard the distant howl of a coyote.

"How appropriate; the sound of loneliness," she whispered to herself. "But probably just my imagination."

Buffalo had been one of the first cities taken by the resurgent USAC, as it moved south from the old Canadian border line. The Rebel Alliance had never bothered to cross it.

Her squads had been on a routine raid of a Buffalo shopping mall. She could remember something hitting her from behind and then waking up in an Attika solitary confinement cell.

"You USACA?" she asked her first torturer.

The uneducated in the Rebel Alliance knew the USAC-CIA, forerunner of the SCIA – Space Central Intelligence Agency – by the abbreviated acronym.

"You'll guess, soon enough bitch!" the masked man replied.

Since she had been a little girl, she had dreamed of that cell; always pitch black, always the feeling of a 'presence' in front of her. She always dreaded a face appearing out of the darkness. It never quite did because she always woke up sweating, usually urinating, before anything happened.

Now she found herself in the real cell – or was *this* even real? She knew it had to be real when her eyes began to make out details of her surroundings. She had been cruelly 'roped' to a wooden chair by an electrical cable, tied around her hands and feet. She noted the plug, still intact, on the cable's end. There were grazes all over her arms legs, and thighs. A pool of blood had formed on the concrete floor between her legs.

She passed out again and only came too when the door opened and the masked man came in, surrounded by a halo of blinding light.

"Feeling better are we?" he began. "Time for a little chat."

After her question about who he worked for, he checked the knot around her wrists. He walked back round to the front and hauled up her blood-stained T-shirt. Somebody had already removed her bra. He stared at her breasts while she struggled to pull away. When the chair began to topple, he steadied it:

"Hey! Bitch! Calm down. Just taking a look at what you got. It could save you a lot of trouble, in here."

"Fuck you! Asshole!"

"Heh! Heh! You should have seen what we did to you while you were *asleep*!"

Muna spat in his face.

"Woo! Hoo! This one's got class! Now suppose you just do two things for me and then we can both get outta here; me to my loving wife and kids, and you to a nice warm cell and hot food. Just tell me a name, any name of a pilot, or *anyone*, involved in the black market freight run to Mars. We know you know someone. A little birdy told us."

"And the other thing?"

"Just fuck me nicely. That's all!"

"Go fuck yourself!"

"Aw! That's not *nice*. And you've got such nice titties. You know, I heard you've got Mexican blood. My daddy used to say that black women like being used. You should always use 'em, he always used to say. And you know what? Spics are just like niggers. Mind you, you have blonde hair, which isn't much like a spic. But then, there are niggers with white hair too, aren't there? Now, are you ready to be nice or do I have to do it my way. You know there's nobody tells me what to do in here. I can do exactly anything I fuckin' like!"

He slapped her viciously across her jaw, wrenching her head to the side and making her head spin.

"Jeez! This is fun!" he continued.

Muna said nothing.

"Okay then. Stew some more. I'll be back."

The treatment became progressively worse. Muna couldn't be sure if they really wanted information or if they just enjoyed inflicting pain. Between a very meagre meal each day, of porridge, a slice of bread and two steel beakers of water, and a short period of sleep, she was tortured mercilessly. They electrocuted her genitals, hung her from the ceiling by her hands, both above her head and behind her back, dislocated both her arms twice, pulled one of her nails out, penetrated her using various brutal objects and put out cigarettes on her the bottom of her feet. The frequent rapes by up to six men, who would then stand around and masturbate on her bloody, bruised body, were possibly the worst episodes.

She survived by shutting off all her emotions and blocking out anything they did to her body. In her darkest hours, she told herself:

"This body is not me. I am in *here* and they cannot get to me! I just have to cut off my feelings and this will come to an end."

To hang on to life became the great enemy. To let her life go and see how the dice rolled became her great solace.

Somehow, her strange power helped her too. She managed to transport herself, in her mind, to green fields and clean mountain air, whenever she needed to. Those green fields were often where she would be when she passed out from the torturer's brutal attentions. And this frustrated him most.

He asked her questions less often. After a while, the attacks, for that was what they had become, became more frenzied, until they reached a climax:

"I no longer care if you live or die!" he told her. "If you don't tell me the answer, I will cut off both your breasts."

She peered out of the only bruised eye that she could still open and saw the burnished blade, swishing in front of her.

But she could no longer remember the question. And her tongue had become so swollen, she could barely get a word out:

"Do it, fucker! Do it!"

He walked around her, perhaps twenty times, but he didn't touch her.

"Fucking bitch!" he muttered under his breath and left.

From that moment on, she knew she would live. She began to cling to life while the tortures grew fewer and less violent. Finally, one glorious day, they dragged her from the cell and dumped her in a clean one, which had water and a bed.

Best of all, when she woke, she saw the sun in the sky.

As she gained strength, they allowed her out into the exercise yard and she began watching for a weakness in the prison's security.

She had once heard an old Rebel telling a story round the camp fire of his escape from a prison.

"The trick … ." he said. "… is not getting out, but having enough time to get away." She saw her chance when she noticed that one of her wardens on the wing left by either of two exits each evening. Muna made sure she kicked up a fuss with all the other warders until they assigned only this warden to her.

Twelve nights later, she overcame the guard, gagged her and tied her into the cell bunk. Muna used the keys to gain the exercise yard. Buildings enclosed the yard, except on the north side, where an eighteen foot wall stood, topped with coils of barbed wire. Using bed sheets tied together, Muna snagged the wire and moments later, dropped to the grass on the other side. She had already spotted the way out from the prson when she made her weekly visits to the bath on the floor above. She dodged between search lights until she reached a gate in the outer wall. She climbed over it, using the now-ripped sheeting to protect her hands from the barbed wire on top and ran, into the night.

From maps she remembered studying before the Rebel raid, she knew a creek lay just a short way to the east. She reached it and waded downstream for almost a mile before heading east again, cross country.

The warden wasn't missed until the following noon, both wing guards saying they thought she must have left by the opposite exit that night. By then, they knew Muna would be long gone. She made a wide circle, around the prison and headed south. Within three days, she arrived back in her camp, hailed as a hero.

Nobody could quite believe that she not only came back but that she had escaped on her own and that her beauty remained intact, some would say enhanced by the scars from Attica.

"We'd given you up for dead!" some said.

"Back from the dead!" said others.

"She's a living legend!" said some.

Soon, that last epithet took hold and Muna's rise towards leader of all Earth Rebels and the title of Desert Princess had begun.

She had a small dragon tattooed onto her back and showed off the scars on her belly and chest proudly. Partly to show off the scars, and partly in defiance, the next time she went into battle against the USAC, she went topless and this would become her trademark.

She remembered all this, and more, before going back to bed. Her scars ran deep. She would never again enjoy sex without needing an element of pain.

***

9 days until Zero Hour

Stone's train had just bypassed the radiation-toxic Las Vegas; last great obstacle before Los Angeles. He woke from a restless night and boarded the train. Today, they would be crossing the last stretch of desert before Barstow. He gave DeTunne a grim look. He could not get a strange voice, and a later strange dream, out of his mind. He felt shaken.

"Jesus! My eyesight maybe not what it was but you look white … as if you saw a ghost!" said DeTunne.

"Ha! Bad night. But got to carry on. Iron in the soul, an' all that?"

"What?"

"Ha! It's a saying... Funny thing is that the Mech-worshippers might be closer to the truth than anyone thought!"

"You're talking in riddles lad."

"There is something tough in our souls... Humans... maybe we're put here for that purpose. The Ischians don't have it..."

"Huh?"

"Listen, what's important is the idea, not the life. My life is of no importance at all. But when I'm gone... Maybe then *you* will be very important!"

"You're not talking sense lad!"

"Pass us that bottle."

DeTunne wiped the neck and passed Stone the bottle of cheap whiskey.

"This … ," Stone said, indicating the bottle of liquor, "… is an illusion! Ha!" He raised the neck to his lips and drained half of the contents in one gulp.

"You're bloody mad!" DeTunne protested, nevertheless impressed by Stone's feat. He raised the bottle to his own lips and took a long swig. Astonished, he held the bottle at arm's length and looked at it askance. "Tastes just like water! Well I'm damned. How the *hell* did you do *that*?"

"Ha! Never mind … . Today we should reach Barstow. Then things might get really tricky. It will be thick with outlaws. And the train will be slow. Watch out!"

DeTunne stood close enough to see that suddenly Stone seemed anxious and had begun to shake.

"Sound like a religious fucker sometimes, Stone!"

"Ha! Come on. Let's go!"

They walked, from the camp near the rear of the train, along its spine, towards the front, jumping each gap between waggons with ease. Most of the men were near the rear of the train, in case they were boarded from behind. DeTunne took up position on the top of the train, ten waggons from the front, while Stone continued forward.

DeTunne would never forget what happened in the next two minutes. Every detail would be etched into his memory like a photographic plate.

Stone had just turned from his position near the engine to give a thumbs-up sign. DeTunne had waved back. He had been enjoying the cooling wind rushing over his face and inside his flapping clothes, as the train reached full speed.

A loud crack, like thunder, cut through the roaring of the wind. DeTunne looked up and saw two huge explosions ahead of the train, beside the track. Great gouts of mud and rock flew up into the air and were quickly shrouded by clouds of dust. Stone disappeared for a moment and then reappeared. He gestured towards the sky behind DeTunne, who turned round and looked up. Two giant Ischian cruisers, yellow striped, swooped down for another shot, aiming their cannons ahead of the train. As DeTunne looked, he saw a flash of painful white light, which scorched the air into red streaks, as two more bursts detonated the plain, close to the track.

"Have to be warning shots!" DeTunne said to himself. He fell to his knees, gripping an air vent desperately. He looked at Stone, who now pointing straight ahead of the train.

"He means to go on. Stupid bastard!"

But then that option suddenly looked completely futile. From high up in the sky, beyond sight, a great beam intersected with the plain half a mile ahead of the train. It created a shimmering wall, stretching high into the sky. The wall had the appearance of the dome shield around Washington. Now DeTunne felt very afraid.

The train continued at full speed towards the force-field wall. If anything, its speed increased slightly. DeTunne saw his life pass in front of his eyes. It took him ten seconds to form any coherent idea in his head. He regretted the two shots of JD whiskey that morning with every frazzled bit of his tortured soul. Just before his plan coalesced, he saw the front of the train impact the wall. Then he saw Stone, now stripped to the waist, jacket tied around him by the sleeves, punching the air with his fists. DeTunne approved of the recently increased musculature of the lad. A strangely calm voice inside his head said, "Like his father... He'll be a good soldier."

But then DeTunne shouted, "No!" Stone disappeared into the crashing maelstrom that the train impacting the wall had become

DeTunne's plan finally crystallised. A voice told him to, "Jump!"

He stood up and jumped to the right, off the train. Just before he blacked out, he knew it would be the last act of a desperate man.

Then he came to. For a moment the pain kept his eyes closed. He opened them and saw dirt in front of his eyes. He lay in a patch of his own blood mixed with dirt in the middle of a hot, dry plain. He lifted his head painfully and looked for the track. It still lay there, about fifteen feet from him. He tried to push himself up with his arms, but one had been broken. Using his good arm, he managed to lever himself up and stood, shakily. He could no sign of the train or the force-field wall or the cruisers. The desert seemed silent, apart from the slight whisper of a breeze through wild grass stems and the distant caw of a crow.

When a local band of Rebels found DeTunne, he tried to explain what happened. Incredulous, they looked for signs of the attack. All they found were two large craters and a fifteen foot long missing section of track. The track, sleepers, ballast, and ground below, for a depth of two feet had been neatly cut away.

They only one item from the train; Stone's jacket lay draped over a rock beside the track.

DeTunne speculated that the energy of the train's motion, and its very substance, had simply been absorbed by the force-field wall. A terror of the technology available to the aliens formed in his heart.

"We can never win!" he yelled, over and over again. During one of his brief, lucid moments, he explained that he worked for Muna. The Rebels, looking for reward, began the long process of returning the broken man to Muna's camp in Utah.

***

8 days until Zero Hour

Kek-suîxjh had been meditating for three hours. At its current speed, the Pet Sounds would pass the anomaly, where he speculated two parallel universes touched, in only thirty three minutes. He wanted to be receptive to any kind of contact he could make with other beings there by using the Path of the Universal-mind.

He came out of his meditation for a moment to check the time on the lounge chronometer.

"Now! It begins!"

He had to restrain his excitement, both scientific and religious, to attain a deep level of meditation again.

When he emptied his mind of all thoughts and concerns about the universe, he saw a wall, like a dark, shimmering diaphanous curtain. It rushed towards him. He passed next to it. Through it, he saw the faces of millions of beings, some like himself. His eyes snapped open. He rushed for an old telescope he kept handy. Pointing it at the universe interface, he took in the strange vision there.

As if on a screen, seemingly hanging in space, images drifted past Kek-suîxjh's field of vision. Some, almost too blurred to decipher, seemed to be of his own Universe. Clearer, were images of worlds he had never seen before.

"But how am I seeing this?"

He looked away from the telescope to think.

"They must be thousands, if not millions, of light years away? Perhaps this really is the information boundary of which some speak. These beings are real, whereas I am but a hologram? Possible…"

He put his eye to the telescope again.

Each face contorted in a rictus, as if the beings were being tortured. Kek-suîxjh wanted to look away. But he wanted to know. He wanted to understand.

"I have to look. Yes, the faces are screaming, some of them crying or looking mournfully into space."

As he watched, horrified, he noticed something else; each being, whatever they were doing, seemed to be moving backwards! He looked more closely. Now he felt sure of it. Many of their activities were unfamiliar to him. Most of the beings looked unlike him. But they were all moving backwards. The pain on their faces seemed very obvious.

"They are trapped in a universe going backwards! They can't escape. Their souls go forward but their lives go backward! How cruel! How horrible!"

The horror of it became almost too great to bear. Kek-suîxjh looked one last time. One of the faces looked straight at him; full of emotion but mostly pathos. The eyes looked mournful for a moment but then the mouth opened in a grimace of abject pain. The lips seemed to be saying:

"Go back! Do not come here. We are in Hell!"

Kek-suîxjh sat frozen in his seat until he had travelled far away from the interface. He felt too shaken to move. For many beats, he sat there; he knew not how long. Then he lay down and slept.

***

7 days until Zero Hour
Alone in J5, I had struggled for two weeks to repair its outer fabric. I had been as comfortable as I could wish in the escape POD 335. I even had recordings of every movie and song available for my entertainment. I still couldn't come to terms with the fact that nearly all their makers would be dead now. I had barely any time to enjoy these luxuries, however. By the time I finished working and retired to the POD, I always felt too exhausted.

I had spent some time during the second day working out what would be a practical first goal in the station's repair. For one man, it would take too long to repair the whole torus. In any case, the fusion reactors on board, if any could be restarted, would not supply enough power to provide all the Oxygen required. The solution had taken me a little while to figure out; make just one small part of the torus habitable.

My first and most critical step had been to repair just the outer fabric for one segment of the great torus, including the solar windows.

My stepfather had been one of the engineers that had built J5. I recalled all the conversations with him as a child, while I swung like a monkey in a suit from the solar window frames. The memories made me smile. Now, I used the special repair-spray tanks I had located in the maintenance depot. Strapped to my back, replacing one of my Oxygent tanks, each of these could spray, through a handheld nozzle, enough transparent seribdenum to cover about fifty square yards. Fortunately, it looked like the aliens had been in too much of a hurry. The damaged areas were relatively small. More damage had probably been caused by floating debris from inside the torus, once it had depressurised.

I picked a segment with the least damage and by the end of the third day, I had made good progress.

"Damn!" I shouted inside my helmet. "Glad I never had to do this as a job!" My sweat had blocked the air-filters. "I can't believe my father did this for a living, the old fart!"

I remembered my stepfather's advice, "Always use a safety-line."

I followed his advice and everything went well until the near the end of another long day. Returning from the maintenance depot with one last fresh oxygen tank, I had only a small section of window left to complete and I didn't bother to attach my safety-line. A movement caught my eye, probably drifting debris, and I swung around, forgetting my weightlessness; a mistake many cadets make. Suddenly I found myself drifting towards a hole in the vast window lattice. If I went through it and out into space I would be lost. I had only seconds to react.

I needed something I could extend, to snag one of the window mullions; long seribdenum h-section struts.

There's nothing!

From nowhere came the distant memory of a training instructor at grunt school.

"If you are detached in space, there are two ways to you might save yourself; detach your air-hose and use it as a jet or, if you are desperate … ."

But I had no time to remember the second option. I yanked on the liquid-seribdenum hose at the base of the gun as hard as I could. On the second try, I ripped it off.

Thank God!

I pointed the jet towards the centre of the hole in the window and began to move slowly back, towards the frame.

It'll be touch and go!

I said a quick prayer. The frame came closer... closer. I kept still, hoping the seribdenum pressure would hold long enough. At the last moment, I lunged for the frame, with the gun nozzle fully extended. It just brushed the frame, swinging me round the outside the window until I collided with it. I scrabbled to get my gloved free hand around something, anything.

Nothing!

Desperate, I rammed the end of the gun between a transparent seribdenum pane and the mullion. I came to a halt, hanging on to the gun.

I heard myself breathing hard. I remained motionless, catching my breath. I had to get back inside before my strength failed. Taking a small rigger's knife from my toolkit, I rammed it into the same gap as the gun occupied, and attached myself to it with the safety-line.

Then I wriggled the gun barrel loose. I rammed it into another gap, right at the edge of the break in the window. Feeding out the line, I hauled myself around the edge of the break and back to the interior of the J-Station. With a huge sigh of relief, I cut the short length of cord and tied the rest of the cord from my belt to a nearby strut.

Safe!

I completed the repair before going back to lifeboat 335.

In that dangerous moment, I had felt more alone than I had even felt on Io when I had nearly died from hypoxia. At least then, I had somebody on the end of a radio and I wasn't a hundred miles from humanity. Here there wasn't anybody for perhaps hundreds of thousands of miles. In a sombre mood, I reflected that I would prefer to die only a few miles from somebody rather than thousands of miles; subtle philosophical point...

The second method of surviving detachment in space, I later remembered, would be to remove your suit and push it away from you. I'm glad I hadn't needed to try *that* method.

The segments of the torus on J5, each about 500 yards long, had a series of guns around the inner circumference. Like the bulkhead doors on an old maritime ship on Earth, during an emergency, these could be fired. This would send a web of seribdenum cords across the diameter of the torus, eventually making an air-tight seal. This would save the occupants in case of an outer hull breach, in theory … . Nobody, to my knowledge, had ever tried it on the full-sized station. My plan involved firing these guns manually.

I couldn't do this, however, until I had restored power, at least for the Station's emergency circuits.

The power to rotate the torus, and thus to create artificial gravity for its 100,000 occupants, came from the solar windows. This was converted into electricity, which in turn ignited Hydrogen gas in hundreds of small thrusters placed around the circumference of the torus in pairs. Each of these thrusters could be angled remotely to allow adjustments to the Station's orbit around the Moon. It made for a very efficient system.

The power for most of the occupant's other requirements came from ten small nuclear fusion reactors. These also replenished the Oxygen supply and provided Helium for the thrusters and other applications, both gases being by-products of the fusion reaction. Water to provide the Deuterium for the reaction normally came from the vast, artificial Golden Gate River inside the torus. Tankers had gradually filled this from the Moon's polar caps during its early years.

The river had gone. When the Station's hull had been breached, and the power cut, the torus would have gradually slowed until all contents not bolted down would have floated out, or conglomerated somewhere inside. I had no way of replacing the water. But I only needed a small amount of water to get the reactors going again. A small amount of Hydrogen had also been harvested from space and held in tanks; I could even use *this* as fuel, if I couldn't find water. Power should therefore be possible and this would produce Oxygen. I would then have a supply big enough to fill even the segment I had sealed off.

The biosphere of J5 had been designed for efficiency but needed a second source of Oxygen. This came from photosynthesis. For this, I needed plants and they usually need Oxygen.

But I had an idea.

When the ship had first been built, the inhabitants hadn't moved in straight away. It had been too expensive to fill the vast inner space with oxygen from Earth. In any case, environmentalists had argued that the vast volume of Oxygen needed for all five stations would seriously deplete the reserves on Earth. So the crops had been planted first on the great farms, which were eventually used to feed the occupants. It had only taken three years for the vast fields of wheat, beet, grasses and wild flowers to produce a breathable atmosphere in ten, air-tight segments. The first Stationites, as they called themselves, arrived and, later, other segments became available, until the whole torus had been filled.

I would find tons of spare grain and other seeds in the Maintenance Depot and these could be planted right around the sealed torus section. Some of them would be strains, genetically engineered from Ischian plants, that didn't need Oxygen. They only needed some Nitrogen-rich soil, sunlight and a little moisture, and *their* by-product *was* Oxygen.

Now that I had repaired the vast windows, the time had come to try and restore gravity. I didn't like to delay my radio message, which would draw any allies to the Station, but I knew I had to make it serviceable, and habitable, before taking the risk of attracting any attention.

In the main Control Room, I found only disappointment. The main control panel had been rendered completely unserviceable; deliberately shot out by laser-fire. The wiring, early 22nd Century stuff that belonged in a museum, had been ripped out of junction boxes.

However, I had an alternative; the Auxiliary Control Room on the Engineering deck. I had even visited it once, on a school-trip.

The auxiliary controls, though basic, were intact. I removed the safety tag with clippers and pulled the big red lever to switch all control to the panel. I pressed the button for Torus Drive Bus to 'On' and heard some clicks, followed by silence. I went back to the 'outside,' inside the torus, and watched for any movement of the window panels against the sun and stars.

There should be some juice in the Station's system.

Finally, after nearly thirty minutes, I saw the evidence, stars vanishing from view, that it had actually started moving, rotating almost imperceptibly slowly.

Yes!

It took only two hours until full 1G gravity had been restored; two terrible hours. From my sheltered position in the main Control Room, I heard many loud bangs and vibrations and watched as debris still inside the torus settled back onto its inside surface. At last, it ended.

Now, I can move more freely.

Quietly pleased to be walking on something solid for the first time in weeks, I made my way back to the Auxiliary Control Room.

My electrical engineering knowledge is basic, to say the least, so I struggled to patch the Torus Drive Bus through to the Main Generator Drive storage batteries. Once this had been done, I made my way to the first of the ten fusion reactors. Nine were basically undamaged, although six months inactivity would most likely have caused corrosion on some components. I had to pull up detailed manuals to even know where to start with them. It quickly became apparent that the task would be beyond me, without help. One mistake, and I risked blowing up J5. I went back to the POD and, for the first time, risked a short databurst laser link with Duffy's receiver on a pre-determined channel. I used Morse code.

When I decoded the reply it said:

> OK. Will take few days to find info. Sorry to inform, Stone killed by alien laser pos. from battleship, nr Los Angeles. DeTunne alive, but non-communicative.

The short message became hard to decode after the word 'killed.' I had to check my decrypt several times. The short message left a hole in the Universe too huge to fill except by an anger that began to burn in my heart.

I staggered to my bunk and lay on it, moaning. My anger at the world kept me in my bunk, not eating or drinking, for two days. I tossed and turned during nightmares and dreams of times together that I would never have with Stone, Katie, Daniel and Mary.

I was alone.

That thought came to me on the second morning and, once I began to accept it, it became possible to open my eyes more. I made a bottle of whiskey using the n-gen and got up.

Only much later that day, did I start to wonder just what the phrase 'non-communicative,' in the message, meant. Had DeTunne became a vegetable? Had he just become a drunkard again? Had he been the only witness to Stone's death? Would I ever know what had happened?

Duffy's replying databurst had the information I needed for the fusion reactors. It also had a few scanned image of somebody's letter. Before studying the documents in detail, I read Duffy's note:

> Attached is a scan of a letter we found today in DeTunne's breast pocket. We think it's genuine.

Bewildered, I read the attached letter:

> Hey dad,
> I had a weird dream this morning. I wanted to write it down before I forgot. I had climbed up this long hill and I decided to take shelter in this cave. But it wasn't a cave but a giant bell and it began to roll. It rolled all the way down the mountain. But then it just kept on rolling; it wouldn't stop. It freaked me out a bit. I don't know why I am writing this to you; I have never written to you before. What I really wanted to say was that I woke up hearing a voice today; just like those strange dreams you told me about when the alien dude first contacted you. You know what? I think it's his friend, Ambi-wassis-name. I can't pronounce it! Anyway, I guess that means I have graduated. I am no longer a

douchebag. I will write more, later, if I get
time. We have almost reached Los Angeles.
Stone

The handwriting and signature looked like Stone's. A
laugh caught in my throat when I remembered he had
been killed. I must have read the letter over a hundred
times, looking for tiny signals; miniscule bits of information. I had to look 'douchebag' up. The definition reminded me, once again, of Stone's fondness for archaic
slang; just one of his little quirks that now cut me to the
quick.

This would be the last communication I would ever
have from my son. I felt alone and the note made me feel
lost again. I knew Katie, Stone and Daniel were dead.
Most probably all others close to me, my mother; my sister, Justine; and my ex-girlfriend Jena, were also dead. I
tried to convince myself that I wasn't alone. Trillions had
probably lost their whole family. There might only be a
few Rebel camps and a few USAC troops left. I tried going about my tasks for a few hours but I couldn't concentrate. Like a cat on a greased wall, my positive thoughts
simply couldn't get any purchase. I seemed to be slipping
into an abyss.

'I need to speak to somebody,' I thought.' The only
person I can communicate safely with is Kek-suîxjh.'

I returned to the POD, emptied my mind and focused
on the Paths of the Universal-mind.

"Are you there Kek-suîxjh?"

I repeated this until it became a mantra. After a long
wait, I heard a reply.

"Yes."

"It's Jake. Are you alright?"

"No. I am in shock."

"Me too."

I heard only silence for a while before Kek-suîxjh continued:

"Why?"

"My son, Stone, is dead."

"Ah. I am sorry. I know what it is to lose a son. I knew about it."

"You did? Yes... yes, I guess I shouldn't be surprised. He left me a letter; at least I believe it's genuine. He said Ambi-xjhu contacted him the morning of his death. At least he was happy to have ... 'graduated,' as he put it."

"Yes. He was a good human. Don't worry. You will see him again. We will all be together soon..."

"Um. I guess so. That brings me peace. I don't know why. But ... but, not too soon, I hope. There are things I have to do. I need to talk to you about those too. But sorry, something is bothering you. What is it?"

"Oh, it's nothing compared with your loss. But... I am deeply disturbed..."

"Go on then..."

"I have found a whole universe that is in ... Hell."

"I don't understand!"

"Neither do I young Jake. Neither do I. I made a pass of an anomaly, what I thought must be the contact point of two universes. I think it was. But those on the other side were trapped in a universe traveling backwards ... in time. It was horrible. It has shaken me badly. Perhaps there really is a Hell. Perhaps there are many Hells. I never did really believe it before somehow. Now I have seen it ... ."

"You saw them? Did you communicate with them?"

"No. They were just ... in pain. One of them screamed at me. I think... Anyway, it's too horrible. I want to reach my destination as quickly as possible. I fear this isolation may drive me mad! Perhaps there is something I can help you with? Ah, I forgot. I have something else I wanted to tell you; Ambi-xjhu has concluded that Stone saw the first moment of time. I disagree of course. Did he ever speak about it?"

"About what?"

"Seeing a butterfly lay her eggs?"

"No."

"Oh. I just wondered."

"Kek-suîxjh. I need to talk about something…"

"Yes. I knew you did."

"I am having a hard time still believing in the Blue Path. Actually, I am having hard time believing in anything! I can't even focus on what I am doing. I know you understand the Blue Path and have some part to play in its propagation and teachings. The Blue Path teaches that I should forgive the Imperial Ischians for their mistake in killing Stone; that it is just naivety on their part. But I can't do it. Katie and Daniel were bad enough … ! Stone is too much! I feel a growing anger. It burns me Kek-suîxjh. If I don't let it out, it will destroy me. A voice inside me keeps telling me one thing; that I must kill the Commander who ordered my son's death."

"Yes … . I fear it is so … for him."

"What? What is so? Are you talking to somebody?"

"Vîu speaks inside me. At least I think she does. I am no longer sure. Perhaps it is my own thoughts. Jake, sometimes base instincts are mysteriously aligned with higher ideals. Your path is to destroy the Ischians, who have violated your world. If anger should drive you to achieve this more easily, you should not question it. Anger is a worthwhile emotion at times."

"I only know that I want to kill."

"Yes. Then go with it Jake. Do not analyse the emotion until you have finished, or the Ischian Imperial Fleet finishes you. It may be only in an extreme state of mind that you can accomplish this thing."

Kek-suîxjh's answer confused me and yet something in it rang true. I fell silent, in consideration.

"You will need to contemplate this Jake. But before you go, you asked Ambi-xjhu for information about the battleship Lu-kshîa and its Commander, A-schian'bakî."

"Yes."

"She is a terrible Ischian; ruthless, wily and ambitious. She has set her mind on subjugating Earth and she has only failed once in her long career. That was when she let your son and his crew back through the wormhole. She will hate humans now. All humans. Your own saying is similar to ours; 'Beware a wounded Ischian.'

"One other thing; I don't know if it's relevant. She is a notorious sexual predator, as most ischians, sorry females, are. And she has a reputation for experimentation ... um sexually. She is probably already experimenting with humans.

"The Lu-kshîa is the first of her class; a ship so vast that it distorts the space around it with its sheer gravitational pull. As I told you before, a second will arrive within days and position itself over the South Pole of your little planet. Together, they will create a field that traps Earth completely. But there is a chance ... a slim chance ... ."

"What?"

"With only two ships, the field will be weak. A fast ship might break through the field at its weakest point; around the equator. That is, it might, until another six of the giant ships arrive to take up station around the equator. However, they are in docks, still under construction. Some may not arrive for another of your Earth years. After that, the invaders will be very hard to defeat. As for weaknesses, these ships have a few; their size; their crews and their drives, which are prone to overheating and breakdown. The Pulse Drive is also unstable at speeds above one quarter the speed of light because of the huge mass of the ship itself, although theoretically it can generate speeds up to twice that. Ambi-xjhu knows this because he actually worked on some of the drive's development. These drives also push out enormous heat and radiation which has to be ducted around complex systems to the outside of the ship. Crews on those decks have short life-expectancies. It might be possible to destroy one of these ships, if

139

you can force them into overdrive. The other method is ramming."

"Thank you, Kek-suîxjh. As usual, you are full of information. I wish you well. I'm not sure I will survive that much longer. I am restarting one of our great J stations. If this is noticed, A-schian'bakî will make short work of me."

"Well, I wish you luck. However, my path seems grimmer. I am not sure which will be worse; having no answers or the answer I may find at the end of this journey. Of course, that is what I will find out. I hardly feel that I care which anymore. I just want an answer that will give me peace when I die."

"I know the feeling of great emptiness Kek-suîxjh. But now I will let my anger in. Perhaps you should take some of your own medicine."

"Medicine?"

"Carry on for Ambi-xjhu, his pups and any others that might survive who have a soul like yours."

"Ha! Your Earth sayings are so amusing sometimes! Good luck Jake."

His voice had suddenly gone from inside my head. I now knew one thing for certain; I would not rest until the captain of the ship that killed Stone had been killed.

I needed technical Information. I struggled off my bunk and continued to work but with a heavy heart.

At last, the first fusion reactor passed the basic pre-start-up tests. I almost didn't care but felt a certain grim relief in moving one step forward. One by one, I started the eight other serviceable fusion reactors. Directing a few thousand gallons of water, which I had found in the freshwater drinking tanks, into the fuel feed lines for the reactors, I started them up. The hydrolysis reactors were the last piece of the puzzle. The fusion reactors would drive these to produce a small amount of Oxygen for the torus atmosphere and Hydrogen as a bi-product. I spent a miserable two days, cleaning out the old tanks and pumps of the hydrolysis system before I could start them. The Hydrogen, I routed back into the emergency reservoir for the Torus Drive.

At last, it all worked and I could take some time for myself, time to do the one thing Stone thought I had come to J5 for. I entered the sealed and isolated segment of the torus; the section containing my mother's house, near the Golden Gates Bridge.

The Bridge itself looked a wreck. Floating debris had become trapped in the suspension cables and the seribde-crete had cracked in many places. It would remain a monument to the past. One thing did, briefly, delight me; where shadow, and cold space, had persisted within the torus, the soil had remained frozen. Now it had begun defrosting so I had many acres of land to grow crops on.

I wanted to use an old tractor to sow them. Later I would sow the other compartments, now that I knew there would be soil there. But that meant doing something first, which I had been putting off: visiting the remains of my mother's house.

With a heavy heart, I donned my suit and set off on a hoverbike to find it. Using an engineering diagram and an old map, I eventually located Mary's sorry husk of a house.

I climbed over the wreckage of decanted jetsam and pushed open the buckled front door. I dreaded what I might find, having already seen thousands of bodies in the torus.

Have to bury those remaining in this segment before they decay.

Pushing through upturned chairs, and other debris, I made my way to the small lounge and pushed open the door. I saw a typical scene of devastation; upturned furniture, books smashed cups and cushions. Even an oriental rug lay draped incongruously over the upturned sofa.

Two things were not typical. The first made me bite my lip. Half under a chair lay the corpse of a black and white dog; Frisky, my mother's old collie. As I bent down to it, I caught the smell of decaying flesh. I pushed the chair off of the body and looked for any clues as to what had happened. I immediately noticed a neat incision between his front legs, about an inch long. I could find no broken bones by touch and there were no other signs of injury. For a moment, I considered taking Frisky's body back with me for analysis but there were too many other bodies that required attention.

As I turned back towards the door, I saw the second unusual thing. Upside down on the wall by the door, in large letters, somebody had written the following message:

> Going to Mars. Love you Jake – Mum and
> Justine xxx

It looked like it had been written using the bright pink lipstick my mother always favoured. I rubbed my glove finger on the writing and put the finger to my helmet's odour sensor. To my surprise, it did indeed have the faint perfume of her lipstick. The subtle smell wrenched back memories and clawed at my heart.

Clearly she had been in a desperate hurry, and gravity had already been lost, when she wrote it. But the message reassured me.

Maybe they're not dead after all!

I would have to analyse things later. I continued on to the garden.

Here, to my relief, I found some soil still clinging to the seribdenum structure, underlying all the buildings on the station. I found the box I had secretly buried when I last visited. I returned to the POD in a sombre mood.

Now I had finished my personal task, I need to start finding recruits.

I opened the box and saw my plastic file with all the codes, frequencies and names of contacts throughout the

Solar System including Gary Enquine and his son, Adam. I had also preloaded them all onto a disk. I only had to slide this into the slot in the POD emergency laser transmitter for an encrypted message to be sent. A secondary message could be sent by radio if I had no response but this would be a dire risk.

Making myself something to eat and drink, I considered what I had found in the torus while I waited for replies.

***

Chapter Four

4 days until Zero Hour

Major Luxmi Davidos awoke, cramped and hot, as she had been for the last seven days. She now felt hungry and dehydrated too.

"And most probably suffering all sorts of side-effects from breathing oxygen-rich air for a few days," she told herself.

The Ischians had quickly worked out how to increase the percentage of Nitrogen in the Station's air supply. Luxmi had looked it up; Ischian biology required about 85% Nitrogen and 12% Oxygen.

Luxmi had quickly needed to run an Oxygen line down the duct from the main oxygen storage tanks just to stay alive. Unfortunately for the Ischians, the Station's recycling units could not keep up for long with this increased volume of Nitrogen. The Ischians had then sealed off the Control Room and supplied the modified mixture only to that room. This resulted in the rest of the Station's air supply being Nitrogen depleted. At first, this had benefitted Luxmi but after a few days, she began suffering; sickness, lack of appetite. Again, a quick trip to the mixture controls had enabled her to survive. Now, she spent almost all her time in the duct, breathing the correct air mixture through a mask. She had been impressed how quickly the aliens were to adapt systems to suit themselves.

'But they're not too *observant*!' she noted. So far they hadn't spotted her own piece of lashed-together tech-adaptation.

The few Ischian grunts who had been left on S.4 as guards, were now based in the main Control Room. They only carried out occasional patrols to the rest of the ship wearing breathing tanks. They had also been fairly successful in switching off all other heating, Luxmi presumed, so that they could increase the temperature inside the Control Room. This allowed her to hide in a duct with warm air; useful when the rest of the station felt like a fridge. The downside was that the Ischians liked their own air *really* hot and this had to go through the ducts.

Luxmi curled up in a ventilation duct near her own cabin. She lay naked apart from the breather. Sweat dripped from her forehead onto the duct floor. Staying close to her own cabin, gave her the opportunity to use the small radio set she had built as a hobby in quiet times. Each day, she had sent out Mayday messages in standard USAC Distress Code or UDC, on the standard frequency. She had rigged the set to record any incoming messages. There had been none so far. She had begun to lose hope.

Stealthily, she crawled to the grate in her cabin wall and waited. She heard and saw nothing for twenty minutes. As usual, she relished breathing without the mask for a short period. Opening the grate, she climbed down to the floor and switched on the com. Streaming the recording to her headband, she played it back. While she listened, she glanced at her reflection in the small mirror on the wall; her short, black hair, pasted to her face. She thought her skin looked pale and blotchy.

I look like shit!

Then she noticed something on the recording; not in the standard UDC but an older one. She had to dig out an old manual to decode it:

> To all survivors. Head for the home of Mary
> Nanden. Use this code to identify. Bring all
> weapons, Oxygen, and water available. Food
> plenty here.

"Yes!" she exclaimed loudly before biting her lip. She danced a little silent dance of joy.

"A rallying call. There *is* life out there!"

'Who the hell is Mary Nanden?' she wondered. The name Nanden certainly seemed familiar.

She struggled almost one hundred yards down the duct before jacking in to a com, to search for the answer. A few moments later, she knew the home of Mary Nanden, wife of the famous robotics designer Douglas R. Nanden. Mary had also been the mother of the highly decorated USAC General, Jake Nanden.

Luxmi felt ready to fight. She wanted to go. The only problem would be transport.

"There are the Escape PODs. But I wouldn't get very far … I have to be patient."

She did some silent stretching exercises and ran on the spot for a few minutes.

"Time to go."

Returning to the duct with food from the n-gen and enough water to get her to the next day, she curled up into the foetal position.

"I have to meditate."

Luxmi and her brother, unusually, had been requested by their new parents as a pair. They were indeed replicant siblings; drawn from the same combination of DNA, and she had no idea who her real parents were. But she knew her adoptive father to be of Indian ethnicity and a Hindu, her mother a Spanish Catholic. Together, they had provided a warm and open environment where religious difference were discussed openly and a cause for celebration and strength. She could draw on the traditional techniques of meditation and prayer to survive. Her faith had always been strong. Now she needed all of it to keep going.

During the night, only indicated by the time on her headband, Luxmi became aware of a change on the Station. It had got hotter. By the time she made her usual short trip to her cabin, she felt seriously dehydrated. Even naked, she still sweated so much that she left wet marks on the ducting when she crawled. Just as she was about to open the grate, she heard, and felt, large feet running in the corridor outside.

'Damn bastards are up to somethin'!' she thought.

Gulping down four filled hip flasks of water from the n-gen, she downloaded the latest log from the old radio. She retrieved another message. It used the standard UDC so she could decrypt it as she read:

> Survivors from S6 Battalion on board Mark 7
> MCS. Identify: friend or foe.

'All my Christmases 'ave come at once! Must act fast.'

"That's why the Ischians are heating the station up. They are preparing for a fight," a voice inside her said calmly.

Luxmi retrieved her laser from just inside the duct, open the cabin door and entered the corridor. She soon found an 'outer' facing viewing port; that is, one facing away from the Sun. She scanned space nervously for the MCS. She spotted it at last; a tiny pale dot, moving across the star-field. She watched it for a while as it slowly drew closer, long enough to know that its trajectory didn't lead directly towards S.4.

She also saw, from the corner of her eye, something she had long suspected would be there from the Station's energy consumption telemetry; an Ischian cruiser. It had attached to one of the Station's five docks on one of the two hubs.

She quickly padded back to her cabin, wondering at the trajectory of the MCS. Were they just avoiding the Ischian's cruiser? Surely if they had seen it, they must suspect the Station was occupied? And if so, they must be desperate and out of power. She had to think of plan, and quickly. She didn't take long to come up with one. Dragging her X.259, and wearing her T-shit and combat trousers, she began the long crawl down the duct.

***

4 days until Zero Hour

"Lieutenant Deitner! Get your men ready for boarding the Station!"

"But..."

"Deitner!"

Colonel Dalgleish's eyes fixed on Deitner as if he were a bore-hole. He learned his first big lesson as a leader; that truth isn't always the best motivator. Through one of the old Mark 7 MCS's viewing ports, he could see that their trajectory was slightly out; they were going to miss Station 4, and also that an Ischian cruiser had already docked on the station's hub. Things looked bad. And yet the Colonel seemed to be planning for a successful outcome, an outcome that Deitner simply couldn't see happening.

'I guess that's why she's a Colonel,' he thought.

"Squad! Check your lasers one last time! Refills! Knives! Breathing apparatus! This may be the last chance we get! Err... We're not just fighting for us ... but the survival of the Solar System!"

Dalgleish patted Hani on the shoulder as she passed. He felt a tingling sensation. He wasn't sure if it felt like love or pride but a moment later, the full reality hit him. He felt sick.

"Listen up, grunts!" Dalgleish began. She waited until the burble of discontented, but excited, troops slowly subsided. "If we're not blasted out of existence by the Ischians in the next few minutes, we will be boarded and eaten for doggy-snacks." She looked around the cabin for dissention. There were only frowning faces. Even the sick men and women were leaning on a friend, suited-up for the final fight. "That is, if we let them! We haven't come all this way to die for nothing. They knew we were coming, have done for days. That means one thing. They're not looking for a fight. They may be drunks. They're probably second rate troops who just want to go home.

Then again, they may want us alive. Either way, it means we have a *chance*! When I give the order, I want squads two, four six and eight to get into the PODs. Throw out anything you don't need. It will be tight and uncomfortable, I know." Pfenigshaven nodded in assent as she glanced at her. Richardson had died on the journey. "We've just transferred the last juice from the batteries into the PODs. It's not much. They were never charged but one of two of them just might reach the Station. If you do, secure it and contact Earth … or any *damned* place. And get things *organised*! If you can take one of these damned cruisers and learn how to fly the sucker, that might be your best bet! I will stay here with the rest of you to co-ordinate things. You sick grunts; if you can hold a laser you'll fight. There is only enough power on board for another thirty minutes. So let's make every second count. We haven't inherited the R-Company tag for nothing! Repos are the best! You... are the best! Now go and do your work!"

Heading for POD 4, Deitner bumped into Baker, the blonde Sergeant with glasses, who had offered him water when he had first reached the Control Room.

"POD 3," the man said, raising his eyebrows.

"Good luck Baker!" Deitner replied, patting him on the shoulder. "See you on the other side... hopefully."

Deitner helped his grunts into POD 4. Meant for a crew of two, the eight man squad could only cram themselves in by tearing out the seats, all extra ammunition cartridges and holding their breaths.

'This is going to be a painful half hour,' Deitner thought, easing another grunt's elbow out of his face.

"Sir?" began one of the grunts. "Why can't the PODs tow the MCS?"

"How the hell would I know, Corporal? From what the Colonel said, there probably isn't enough juice left in this thing to light a cigar!"

"Seal the hatches!" Dalgleish ordered. "Keep tethered until the last moment!"

Moments later, Deitner's POD detached. Red light blinked on and off on the various control panels, although the bodies were too tightly packed for anyone other than the trained pilot to know see anything outside. She called out the distance from the MCS.

"Seventy yards, eighty yards … ."

"How much fuel?" somebody asked.

No answer came. Deitner could only hear the sound of heavy breathing and somebody's piss dripping onto the metallic floor pan. Any moment he expected to see a bright flash.

'They say that is all you know of your death,' he mused.

His mouth had curious metallic taste in it and his bladder felt very, very tight.

"Two hundred yards … and ten … ."

At the same moment, Dalgleish also wondered when the bright flash would come. And then she saw it; a flash of white from one of the Ischian cruiser's flank laser. It would be the last thing she ever saw.

***

4 days until Zero Hour

Luxmi Davidos reached the huge recycling storage tanks. Here, close to the Station's axis, the artificial gravity reduced so she occasionally floated off the bottom of the duct while she crawled.

"No guards! Arrogant bastards! Ha!"

She quickly turned the Nitrogen master cock to -20 and the Oxygen master cock to +20. She had expert knowledge of the system; as far as the Ischians would know, the gauges would still read the correct mixture. It would take them some time to figure out what was going on and they would probably be unconscious by then. Even so, she had to take into account the the cruiser crew.

Pulling the Air-Conditioning Station Plan up onto her headband, she began the long crawl to the Auxiliary Control Station, deep in the guts of the great disk. The ducts formed a maze of tight corridors and it took her nearly an hour to reach her destination. She sweated heavily but at least she could breathe an Oxygen-rich atmosphere. Its blast made her feel high and crave chum. Reaching a sealed panel, she unlocked it using a special key only a few members of the crew held, and dropped to the floor of a tiny cell. It lay away from any corridors. In front of her, in the dark, she saw a panel of flashing lights. Locating the docking control panel, she changed the Primary Security Over-ride Code using a complex procedure and then set all the docks to permanently lock. This would over-ride any local attempts to dock or undock.

"Ha! Now let's see you use that cruiser, you alien bastards!" A shockwave that threw her off her feet interrupted her glee.

"Oh! Oh!"

Then she heard the sound of heavy, running feet.

'Hm. Going for the station defence lasers,' she thought. 'Okay, no problem.' She flicked the power switch for the defence lasers and they instantly went dead. "Better seal the Control Room now too!" She punched another switch. For good measure, she cut the power supply to the cruiser. If the aliens were their usual crafty selves, they would already have fitted a voltage adaptor to the docking assembly and tapped into the Station's grid. Unable to undock, it would take the a few minutes to disentangle themselves from a trap of their own making.

Checking that the torch in her pocket flashed properly, she crawled to a nearby storage room, opened the grate and dropped to the floor. She cautiously opened the door and looked both ways down the corridor.

'Nothing coming.'

She quickly went to the nearest outer viewing port and looked for the MCS.

'It's not there! Shit! No, wait! What's that?'

She could see only debris from the destroyed MCS, at first, but then out of the debris field emerged two specks. "PODs!" She flashed a message using the torch in Morse code.

Go to Rear Dock 5. Do not acknowledge. Ischians onboard.

It took a few moments, but then both PODs altered course. Checking for aliens at every corridor intersection, she made her way to Dock 5. On her way, she noted, with satisfaction, that there were no longer any lights on in the cruiser windows. She quickly punched in the new Override Code and primed her laser.

****

4 days until Zero Hour

Lieutenant Hani Deitner thanked his God, Mech, that he hadn't been in the two PODs on the outer side of the MCS. Having needed to negotiate their way around the MCS, they were caught in the explosion. He could see no sign of them through his tiny portion of the viewing port.

"How far to go?" he asked the pilot, trying to sound calm. He felt his teeth start to chatter.

"One hundred and twenty yards... sir!"

'We'll never make *it*!' Deitner thought.

"Good," he said. "Is the other POD still with us?"

"Err. Yes, but drifting, Sir, I can see something flashing in one of the Station's ports!"

"Let me look. Move soldier!" Deitner pushed two grunts aside to get to the main port; what served as a windscreen. He stared at the bright white light.

"Flashing irregularly," he said, thinking out loud. "Code mebbe … . Anybody know any standard codes? Sergeant Pfenigshaven, can you take a look?"

Bodies jostled and rearranged themselves while Pfenigshaven struggled to the port.

"Oh yeah! It's Morse code. Learned it once. Shit! Never thought I might use it. This is *real* old school … . Wait. It says, 'Go to Rear Dock … five,' I think. 'Do not acknowledge. Ischians on board,'"

"You think … ?"

"Yeah. Dock 5. That's over there!" She pointed to the rear of the slowly spinning S.4.

"Let's *go* there!" said Deitner, almost shouting. He gripped the base of the pilot's stool as if it were his own life, ebbing away. "Why the hell aren't they shooting at *us*?"

"Sir! The power must have gone out on the cruiser. Look!"

"Okay. We may only have this one chance. How much more juice?"

"None! We're coasting! Shall I detach the tether?"

"What? Er. Wait … ." Deitner looked out of a rear port, to where he could see the other POD. Pfenigshaven's face joined his and they both nodded. "No." Three hundred meters of tether trailed behind Hani's POD. The tail-end has been torn off in the explosion, sending the POD off course, but the pilot had been able to correct. The other POD hadn't been so lucky. Already out of fuel, they were now drifting away from Dock 5 on an oblique course. "They might just have a chance... Get me the other POD." He spoke into the transmitter microphone. "POD 4 to POD 3. EVA now! All of you. In about thirty seconds, the end of our tether will reach you. After that, it will be too late! If one of you can grab it..."

"But sir! It's … ."

"I know! I know! It's a risk we have to take!"

"Roger!" came the reply from POD 3. Deitner kept the channel open and could hear the desperate efforts in the stricken POD to get a man outside with a tether attached. As the seconds were counted down to ten, it looked like they wouldn't make it. At the last moment, the hatch opened and a suited man launched himself out, pushing off from the POD to the tail of the snake passing by. He grabbed it and simultaneously another man emerged from the hatch, attached to the other end of a short tether

"No!" yelled Deitner. "That's only two men!"

"We're more likely to make it though." observed Pfenigshaven, wryly.

With two men only attached to the tether, POD 4's course deflected less. But as the pilot had feared, the uneven weight on the end of the line still sent them slightly off course. Now they had their own problems. For a minute, they watched POD 3 floating away into deep space, to be lost forever. Deitner hoped Baker was one of the two men on the tethered line.

"Okay Sergeant. What do we do when we hit, I mean impact, the Station?"

"Well... I dunno sir. We're gonna miss the hatch … that's fer sure, but not by much. We still had power after the explosion so we *were* on course … ."

"Sir?" chipped in Sergeant Pfenigshaven.

"Yes?"

"We EVA and tie ourselves to the Station. We then drag or tow the POD to the hatch."

"Okay... Yeah. That does it for me. Four to EVA. Two to stay inside. I guess that's you and me, pilot."

Luxmi Davidos saw the POD hit the Station, just outside her viewing port next to Dock 5. She saw four grunts attach tethers to the station and then, painfully slowly, as if in some old slow-motion film, drag the old POD into position over the dock. Two men held grab rails either side of the POD and slammed it against the dock several times until the catches caught and hydraulic hammers drove the POD firmly into place. She waited while the four suited men regained the POD and re-pressurised it. At any moment, she expected the Ischians to power up the cruiser and open fire. Breathing hard, she tried to be patient.

"Boy, are we glad to see *you*!" said a tall, brown haired Lieutenant with a goatee beard, stepping out of the docking hatch. She took his hand. It wasn't the beard that shocked her but the emaciated state of the men when they emerged.

"Me too Lieutenant I think I'm the only one left aboard; *human*, that is. But we haven't got much time. The Ischians will power up the cruiser any second. They won't be able to use the docking hatch because I sealed it after changing the code. Even *they* are not *that* clever! It won't take them long to find a way in though. We're gonna have to fight them. I've gassed the ones in the Control Room; about ten, I would guess. There were a few more running around but I don't know where they are; probably trying to sort out the air-mixture. It's Oxygen-rich right now, which they don't like!"

Deitner took a moment to take all this in. He blinked. "Okay. But the men in the other POD..."

"Yeah... We got no time. Later, we might be able to do something. Right now, I need two men. The rest of you are going to have to hold the fort while we find the aliens and deal with them. Dock Three is where they will come out, if they can get the dock open. If not, who knows..?"

"Okay. You two, Go with her," Deitner order two grunts. "The rest, follow me!"

As they ran, Davidos looked at the two men with her. "You look like shit! Emaciated! What the hell happened?"

"Combination of malnutrition, bad air and lack of sanitation for two whole months!" one of them replied. "Quite a few dead; those with wounds didn't stand much of a chance,"

They found two Ischians right where they expected, at the recycling storage tanks. Turning the corner, the USAC grunts opened fire first. One of the aliens had his helmet off, long ears placed close to a valve. He died instantly with a shot from Luxmi's laser. The other swung round at an almost impossible speed and opened fire. In the lead, Luxmi leaped to one side and found the shelter of the corridor corner just in time. The two grunts from the MCS were not so fast. Both were hit and sprawled in front of Davidos.

She dropped to the floor behind the bodies of the grunts and opened fire. For a few seconds, one of the grunts held down the trigger of his laser with his remaining arm. A red beam played randomly across the roof and wall, hitting neither Ischian. Then the beam fell to the ground. The grunt lay dead.

'Two against one! Not good!'

Luxmi ran. She felt something wet on her thigh. She looked down. She had been lucky but, even so, a small sliver of her thigh had been sliced off.

'Jesus!' she thought to herself. 'If this is what it's gonna be like, we don't stand a chance!' She made for one of the small ordnance stores. 'Maybe they haven't found them, or haven't bothered … .' she thought. She punched in the new code and the thick, armoured door swung open. She stepped inside and grabbed three grenades, just in time. Hearing heavy footsteps behind her, she swung round at the same time as pressing a grenade firing button in the correct current USAC sequence. She didn't even wait for the red, flashing warning light before throwing the grenade. The Ischian knew that the object would blow its head off. But it stood too tall to reach down for it in time; the grenade went straight past its legs. In an almost comic gesture, it tried to kick the grenade and kicked the wall instead, grunting once.

The huge explosion threw Davidos fifteen feet back down the corridor, covering her with a shower of combined suit and body parts. Pale orange blood dripped down the walls and down her cheek.

"Sucker!"

She grabbed a crate of grenades and ran to the Control Room hatch. Peering in, she counted eleven Ischians lying unconscious in various poses.

'Sleeping like babies!' Luxmi mused.

Then she ran back to Dock 3.

She met Deitner and four grunts, running the other way.

"They're out. Outside! Coming in through the roof!" Deitner yelled. "This way!"

The sound of rushing air followed a muffled explosion. Davidos knew the Ischians had blasted a hole through the outside of the Station.

"Oh shit! I've got no air!" she shouted.

"Get some! Fast! We'll hold 'em!"

"Here! Grenades!" She grabbed three for herself and dropped the crate. She ran down a side-corridor to get what she needed from an old mate's quarters.

The rushing of air stopped, which meant the aliens had somehow sealed themselves inside the outer skin of the station. However, all the air in the surrounding corridors had now been sucked out through vents and fissures in the roof. A blast of trapped air hit Luxmi in the face when she opened the cabin door. She gulped it down and held her breath.

'Now there will be *nothing* to breathe!'

Pulling the air tanks and mask on, she started the air flow. Out of breath, her lungs screamed for air. At last she felt the cool flow of Oxygen on her face and gulped it in. She started back to the battle. She had no time to adjust the harness and the tanks slapped against her kidneys, making her feel sick. All the time, the air got thinner.

Reaching the scene of the battle, she saw that she had arrived too late; the Ischians were already inside. At least, most of them were. Deitner and the last grunts were firing at the alien legs as they emerged through the hole in the corridor roof. The hole lay between the USAC troops and the Control Room.

"Shit! Another detour!"

She went back to the corridor and crossed to the other side of the hub before setting off again in the direction of the Control Room. When she thought she had gone far enough, she cut back to the original corridor. She could hear laser-fire, so she waited.

Luxmi heard heavy footsteps approaching. She took two grenades and pressed the sequence. Two red lights flashed at her. Waiting until the counters both said '1 second', she peered around the corner and threw them. The Ischians were surprised. Four of them stopped in their tracks, the rearmost already holding a wounded arm. They were all stooping to stop the top of their helmets from scraping the ceiling. One of them dropped to his knees, as if praying. Then they were gone, in a mist of biomium spacesuit, orange blood and fur-covered flesh.

'They call that; evening the odds! Bastards!' she told herself.

Then Davidos had a momentary feeling of ennui. She shook her head, and ran past the body parts and bloody walls, towards the battle. She pointed her laser barrel down the corridor.

When she arrived at a corner onto the corridor, Deitner and three grunts were battling the last four of the Ischians who had climbed through the hole. The body of a dead soldier lay in front them, with a pool of blood around its head. Deitner and a Lieutenant lay prone behind the body. Behind them were the two other soldiers.

The four Ischians were arrayed, crouching, in front of the hole, as if protecting it. They waited for more aliens but help didn't come.

"I have only about three seconds left!" Hani said over the intercom.

He fired a single laser pulse. A blinding white streak of light cut air to the rightmost Ischian. The alien barked and grabbed its chest. It crawled behind its neighbour. The second alien moved over to cover the wounded Ischian.

The white laser light surprised Luxmi. She glanced at Hani's laser rifle and saw the clover leaf logo for the first time.

'Jeez! We have a chance!' she thought.

"We have *grenades..*!" she yelled.

"Only four left!" Hani answered.

"Sixteen grenades to a box; that's twelve grenades," Davidos yelled. "You can't have used them all!"

Deitner's other grunts ignored her and pumped endless bursts of laser-fire into the aliens' suits, which absorbed it all.

But then she looked at the last aliens. They were kneeling in a pile of gore. Their normally grey suits were bright orange. Clearly the grenades had been deployed usefully. About thirty yards apart, and with a mist of smoke, blood and vapourised flesh filling the corridor, neither side could clearly see their targets.

The tallest Ischian suddenly stood up to get a better aim and opened fire. Trying to shield Deitner and Pfenigshaven behind him, one of the front-most USAC grunts also got to his feet. His body instantly absorbed a blast of the white-hot alien laser-fire and exploded. The grunt beside him got to his knees and howled before pressing the trigger of this laser. He held it down while a red bead glowed on the standing Ischian's belly. The alien fired at the grunt's head, but he dodged the shots, moving his head this way and that. He held down the trigger. After a few seconds, at the limit of the laser's heat cycle, the red dot became a hole. The surprised alien looked down at the puff of smoke from his own flesh. Now the heat had penetrated, the contents of his torso. This heated up within a half second and created a small explosion which erupted from the Ischian's belly. There was now a football-sized chunk of flesh missing. The alien fired one more haphazard arc of white light and collapsed over a dead carcass. The USAC grunt's finger remained on the trigger while he keeled over. The top of his helmet and head had been neatly sliced off.

"Throw me a grenade!" Luxmi yelled.

Deitner reached into the box and lobbed one to her.

"Remember your high school sports days," she told herself. "This is for the trophy!" She took a deep breath. To reach 90 feet would not be impossible in open air, but in a narrow, low corridor it probably would be.

"Now!" Hani yelled. He and the last two soldiers, Pfenigshaven and one other, opened fire with everything they had left. But Hani's laser stopped dead in his hands after a half-second burst.

Luxmi stepped out into the corridor and, at the same time, lobbed the heavy grenade as straight and hard as she could. They all followed the dark object with their eyes as it flew, spinning through the red mist towards its target. But at the top of its arc, it hit the ceiling and dropped to the floor ten yards short. Luxmi held her breath as the grenade spun round and round, skittling towards the enemy. The last two aliens were transfixed too. Their own death spun only a fraction of a second away. The grenade stopped only a yard short of its target. There followed a moment of complete silence. Then the corridor erupted. Through the resulting red, wall-spattering mist of flesh, Luxmi and the others watched for the results. When the smoke cleared, only the wounded alien still remained, crouching behind the other smashed bodies. With a gaping chest wound and a missing arm, she didn't have long to live. She stood up and held up her laser rifle. Its barrel had been bent and the chamber smashed.

The Ischian looked almost pitiable as Luxmi pressed the ignition sequence and threw the last grenade. The alien raised its arms in surrender just before it disappeared into alien oblivion.

"Okay. Okay. Back to Dock Three," Luxmi said over the intercom.

At the dock the four soldiers left guarding the hatch were leaning against the wall.

"They're not coming out!" one of the grunts declared. "Either they can't. Or won't!"

"Alright, what now Lieutenant Davidos?" asked Deitner.

"Seal the leaking section and then to the Control Room. You're gonna have to help me. They're all sleeping like babies but *I* don't want to kill 'em all. Deitner and the others looked at each other."

"You stay here!" Deitner told the four guards.

When Davidos, Deitner and the remaining grunt reached the hole again, a quick inspection led Davidos to conclude that the hole would be too big to fix.

"Just seal the corridor," she said. "There are bulkheads every one hundred feet. You'll find a pair of blue levers. Just pull the furthest one and wait for me. Don't forget to stand *outside* the bulkhead!"

Davidos typed in the security code herself to seal the first bulkhead and led them round the corridors to the second.

"Five minutes. Ten at most. The system automatically detects bulkhead activation and increases the flow outside that section."

She left for the Control Room. When the second bulkhead sealed, the air pressure began to increase.

In the Control Room, the aliens were still unconscious. Luxmi punched in the over-ride code on the key pad and the hatch 'swished' open. Deitner, Pfennigshaven and the other grunt arrived.

"Okay. I see thirteen. That's three each and one extra for me!" announced Deitner.

The others looked at him. "I'm being kind," he added. He pulled the helmet off the nearest Ischian and fired a half second burst into the base of the skull, sweeping it sideways to sever the spinal cord. "Quick, and painless," he said.

Davidos did the same, although her two Ischians weren't wearing helmets.

When they finished, they turned around and saw Pfenigshaven hesitating. "Come on, soldier. We can't take prisoners." Pfenigshaven had been just about to fire when Davidos held up her hand.

"Hold it! We need at least one alive if we're gonna take that cruiser!"

"Are you crazy?" asked Deitner.

"No Lieutenant. I'm not. Yesterday I got a message from J5, you know, the big civvy station? There's somebody there. It's a rallying point. We have to go. Where else can we go? And if we're going there, we need transport. What's more, a cruiser kind of evens the odds, doesn't it?"

"Okay. I suggest two aliens. Or maybe three. How do we know which one can fly the thing?"

"Good point, Lieutenant. I suggest the shorter two. They're probably no good as fighters so more likely to be pilots." She fired the last shot into the skull of the tallest remaining alien. When she looked up, Deitner was looking at her strangely. "Yes?"

"Nothing. What is your rank anyway? With only that T-shirt on, I can't tell."

"Does it matter? We need to think how to get into the cruiser. Let's bring these two round."

"Yeah. Right now I need to get after that POD. I'm not *giving up* on it."

"Sorry Lieutenant. It will take days to get this thing started. By then, they will be long dead."

"But I have to..."

"Don't worry. I have an idea. The Maintenance POD. They might have messed with it so it's risky."

"I'll go on my own. Is it difficult to … fly?"

"Nope. Any fool could control it. But you will need somebody to help you grab the POD. I better come."

Hani ignored her. "Sergeant. You can fly a military POD so you should be able to handle this?"

"Sure sir. No problem."

"Okay. Show us the way … er … ?"

"Major. Major Davidos."

"Oh. Shit! I mean sorry sir," replied Deitner, turning red.

"Don't worry. I was only Ops. Room fodder until now. You guys do all the hard work!"

"Well, I was only a private until a few weeks ago."

"Yeah. How things change!"

They pointed the Maintenance POD, or MP, at the tiny blip on its radar screen. By now, POD 3 had drifted almost one hundred miles away. With the MP's thrust at full power, it took the rescuers almost four hours to catch it. Fortunately, its course had intersected the orbit of the Station and they would not have much further to go back.

When they could finally see the POD with naked eyes, Deitner let out a long sigh of relief.

The sergeant pilot used the MP's grabbing arms to swivel the military POD around, bringing its hatch in line with the MPs' own so that they could open the hatch. Out climbed four weary and semi-conscious grunts.

"Boy am I glad to see you!" said Baker, his lungs heaving for breath. "A few more minutes and I think we would have been gone. One hour tanks!"

***

Back on S.4, Davidos and Deitner headed for the docked alien cruiser.

"By the way, Major, I meant to ask; what happened to your hair?" Hani pointed to her right ear

"What?" Luxmi put her hand to where hair had once covered her ear. She could feel none there. "I thought my hearing had improved! Must have been a shot from an alien at the tanks. That's when I lost your two men."

"Suits you, slightly … ."

"They ain't coming out," declared one of the four grunts guarding Dock 3. "We figure there's only two left. They sealed their external hatch and we hardly seen a thing of 'em since then."

"Oui!" said one of the others, nodding.

"I have an idea!" Luxmi announced.

She had the two aliens from S.4s Control bound with electrical cable and revived. They were led to Dock 3.

"You know what to do," Davidos said into the throat mike, which translated her speech into guttural Ischian instantly and amplified it.

The taller of the two cable-bound Ischian captives nodded. They had been surprisingly quick to co-operate once they became conscious and found a laser pointed at their heads. Both said they were low-ranked.

"Can either of you fly that cruiser?" she asked through the translator. The taller one nodded uncertainly, while the smaller one had just blinked. "Terrific. Okay, you want to live and go back to Isch-su?"

The taller nodded quickly again, the smaller had blinked again and then said something. The translator told her the alien came from Bek-su.

"You are going to persuade your friends to come out," Luxmi suggested. "We will give them the Maintenance POD when we leave here, before we destroy the station. Boom!" She added the last word for clarity. The translator struggled with it but the aliens understood.

At Dock 3, the taller Ischian stepped up to the com panel and spoke in his guttural language.

He explained that five large charges had been placed on the bottom of the cruiser's hull and would be detonated in one hour if they didn't bang on the docking hatch and then come out, naked and with their paws held high. A few minutes passed before Luxmi heard a clanging sound on the other side of the hatch. The USAC troops were ready for a trick but the two Ischians came out wearing nothing. Both were tall. The taller wore copious amounts of jewellery; a female. Davidos looked away in revulsion at their genitals. Deitner looked horrified; fascinated. By the way in which the shorter Ischians deferred to her, Davidos knew the taller alien to be the commander. Both were bound and locked in a cell with the two from the Control Room.

Davidos, Deitner and the others cautiously went inside the cruiser. Everything looked oversized, including the seats, made for bodies up to ten feet tall.

"We have to get out of here, now!" Davidos announced. "They will have sent a distress call. It won't take long!"

"But can we fly this thing sir?" asked Deitner.

"Cut out the 'sir!' Well, it doesn't look like it's changed much."

"From what?"

"Well, I had plenty of time to study Ischian cruiser technology while I was hiding," she replied. She ran her hands lovingly over the unfamiliar panels and switches. "I *had* thought of drawing them all out, except maybe a guard, which I could overcome, and then stealing it. Fortunately, there is some data available on how to fly these things, at least ones built a few years ago. That Stone Nanden, the kid that went through the worm-hole? He saw one damaged in a deep space battle this side of the worm-hole he jumped through. The aliens were careless enough to leave the wreck, which the USAC recovered later. They eventually rebuilt it, flew it and wrote some kind of basic pilot's manual for it. The manual only includes basic stuff, like how to turn down the light intensity, temperature, and how to navigate through sub-space. Matter of fact, we reverse engineered a lot of the tech stuff for our latest models of cruisers."

"But can you *fly* it sir?"

"Well … probably … with some help from our little furry friend."

"Why not take the commander. She must know how to fly it?" asked Baker.

"Too risky. Too strong. There would be trouble. Okay, I reckon we should give it fifteen minutes. No more. We need all the stores we can get on board; I'll show you where to get them. We need two n-gens: I know where the best two are. And I am gonna rig S.4 to explode in one hour. That way it might even take some of the new arrivals with it. Don't tell the prisoners. Oh yeah, and two of you get them into the MP. It won't have juice for more than an hour but that doesn't matter. Now, two of you come with me. The rest get back here at … ." She checked the time in her headband display. "02.17."

The four Ischians made a comical sight, squeezing their huge bodies into the small Maintenance POD. With two minutes to go, Luxmi Davidos had just finished rigging the main Nitrogen and Oxygen tanks to explode, when she heard a tapping sound beside her. She had already sent the last grunt back with some tools so she was alone. She grabbed her laser to defend herself.

Luxmi stood next to a small grubber tank, filled half way with liquid around a rocky island. "Oh God, I had forgotten about you! Why the hell did you have to emerge right now! Now I will have to take you too!"

She grabbed an old oily towel and lifted the lid of the tank. Scooping out the cat-sized, grub-like, creature, she wrapped it in the towel and stuffed it under her arm.

"Who knows? You may be the only life-form from Earth alive, besides us, when this is all over! Time to go!"

The cruiser hatch shut behind her, right on the fifteen minute mark.

"Hold this!" she said, handing one of the grunts the wriggling bundle.

"What the hell is it?"

"A grubber. 'Genetically-engineered Recycling Utility Bio-organism'; a creature that can live in air, water, gasoline; just about anything. Used to keep pipes clear and clean. It's a recent addition to the Station."

"What do I do with it?"

"Stash it in a storage unit for now."

The grunt put the bundle in a storage unit made of biomium, a biological version of plastic used by the Ischians.

"It'll be okay in air for a while, but we need to put it in water soon," Luxmi continued. "Don't worry, it will clean the water for us; it will clean anything."

"Genetically engineered from what?" Deitner asked.

"God only knows. Anyway, no time to explain now. We gotta go. Where we goin'?"

"J5, you said."

They could see the Maintenance POD, heading off as fast as it could go, in the opposite direction.

***

4 days until Zero Hour

"Now!" whispered An-Hnadhîa to the small Ischian lying prone beside him. "Don't forget; back in three hundred beats!" he added as they both sped onto the moonlit battlefield at the Rebel Princess's camp.

An-Hnadhîa and his driver had been the only two left on the bridge of the J-Crawler. By an incredible stroke of luck, An-Hnadhîa had glanced at the ground radar ten seconds before the giant mine exploded beneath the vehicle. They had already detected the tunnels, too late. He had already ordered all his remaining crew to escape, to fight for their lives before the J-Crawler became over-run while he had stayed with his driver to try and save it. But then he had seen the mine, blinking neon blue on the screen.

Designed to save pilots, which were expensive to train and who always stayed on board until the last moment, two ejector seats were fitted to the new Class 5 J-Crawler. An-Hnadhîa had often gone over what he would do in just such a situation; he had no intention of sacrificing himself for the High Council.

"Press the self-destruct pad and strap yourself in!" he barked to the pilot. "Eject on my command!"

The small Bekian pilot hit two buttons at the same time without hesitating. Two straps over his chest tightened and an Ischian voice announced, "Self-destruct in ten beats … . Nine, eight, seven … ." An-Hnadhîa jumped over the back of the chair and started strapping himself in. "… six, five, four, three, two … ." An-Hnadhîa nearly dropped the belt before he could secure it. He had no time to check if it was properly locked. The driver hit another button and it pulled tight.

"Now!" the Commander bellowed.

The terrified driver punched the eject button and compressed gas canisters fired the two seats through an ejected hatch in the roof of the bridge, an instant before the J-Crawler erupted in a ball of fire. Curved-bar frames sprang out and around their chests, like rib cages, to protect them. Around the two Ischians, the air became a hell of flame and hot gas. Their fur singed and the air inside their noses, throats and lungs seemed to ignite. But somehow they emerged from the top of the fireball and started to fall to earth, behind the crater where the vehicle had been. Hydraulic jacks extended from the cage brackets to break their fall; not an ideal solution but the Ischian body is very tough. The cages bit into the desert dirt before rolling slightly and coming to a stop. The wind had been knocked out of both Ischians. The alien troops around them were too busy trying to stay alive to help.

An-Hnadhîa punch the cage release and then the harness release before the driver moved. The big alien fell flat on his face in the dirt but he didn't care about the indignity; he was alive. Without waiting to catch his breath, An-Hnadhîa stood up and ran towards the southern edge of the battlefield. He didn't notice the Bekian following him, dodging between shell explosions and enemy laser-fire. An-Hnadhîa grabbed a laser from the body of a fallen Ischian grunt just before he reached a small clump of dry bushes.

There they hid both for a while before retrieving two sets of respirators. Then they crawled further into the brush to wait until nightfall.

Now he had survived almost certain death An-Hnadhîa had one small problem; air. They could breathe normal Earth atmosphere for a few hours but after that, they would become dizzy, progressively weak and listless before eventually suffocating. They needed a supply of respirators from the battlefield before the humans took them.

In darkness, the Ischian Commander led the smaller driver on to the battlefield.

An-Hnadhîa returned to the scrub, dragging six sets, the Bekian, four.

"Just my luck to be stuck with a Bekian! Mem-chu, isn't it?" An-Hnadhîa said, panting.

"Yes Commander!"

"You needn't sound so optimistic. We have very little chance of getting out of this. I would rather... die with an arrogant fool than a slimy obsequious worm like you!"

Mem-chu said nothing.

"Listen Mem-chu. As you know... I don't like *you*! Not only are you a Beckian colonial runt but you were a political placement; forced on me by my superior. But we are going to have to work together if either of us are going to have any chance of surviving. If you can't, I will simply kill you and probably eat you."

An-Hnadhîa knew A-schian'bakî very well. He knew she would be angry at the death of her favourite sex-toy but she would not waste any of her forces on a large effort to search for him. Eminently pragmatic, she had become the darling of the Imperial High Council and the scourge of all her underlings. He had never liked her. But being a practical Ischian male, a career soldier, he knew how to survive in an oppressive regime. For the sake of his wife and two pups, he put up with hours of humiliation in A-schian'bakî's cabin. He didn't like to remember some of things she had made him do. He steeled himself for yet another challenge.

"I can't have excess baggage. Is that clear?"

"Yes Commander."

"Good. Now, this air will have to last us as long as possible. After that, we are dust. Every Ischian suit has a homing device, as you know, but it's effective only up to distance – oh, from here to those mountains. I know my Commander well, very well. I don't think there will be anybody out looking for us. We are on our own."

An-Hnadhîa decided they would hide in a small copse, for as long as their air lasted, or until he could think of a way to be rescued. They survived on the meat of any local fauna they could kill with their lasers.

After two weeks, their air supply had become almost exhausted.

***

4 days until Zero Hour

Half way to J5, Major Luxmi Davidos and her men were relaxing on the Ischian cruiser.

"No sign of anything on this crazy Ischian radar sir!" reported Pfenigshaven.

"Okay Lieutenant. Stand down for half an hour. First watch! You're on again. Is there any more of that cream pie stuff in the food locker? I dunno why Ischians don't have n-gens yet, and God knows what's in it, but *I like* that stuff!"

Sitting by a port, staring into space over the creamy alien concoction, Luxmi's mind completely switched off. She only became aware of someone talking when the voice rose almost to a shout. Then it became a scream. She spun round to see the taller alien holding one of the new LC5150 Bullpup laser carbines to Pfenigshaven's head. The alien snarled something, staring aggressively at Luxmi.

"Put it down," Luxmi said calmly. She lowered her arms to indicate what she wanted the alien to do. The Ischian snarled again. "What happened Lieutenant?" Luxmi played for time, always moving a little closer to the alien. The smaller one still squatted on the far side of the taller Ischian.

"I don't know sir. I was just fixing myself a drink. The two aliens were still tied up, as far as I could see. Then, suddenly this one jumped up and grabbed my carbine from its holster. I don't know how she did it!"

"Okay. Stay calm. They just want to live. No doubt they think their own kind will kill them if they don't make *some* kind of attempt to escape. Now they *have*, they probably just want it all to calm down again."

Davidos now stood only ten feet from the alien. The Ischian barked something and waved the LC5150 menacingly.

'Maybe she will use it,' Luxmi decided. She stopped. "Anybody got a translator?"

"Nothin on board!" yelled Baker. "I made an inventory of everything … unless there is one built into a console…"

Davidos held her throat between her finger and thumb; an attempt to signal what she wanted. The Ischian seemed to understand and edged Pfenigshaven towards the flight deck.

'This is dangerous,' Luxmi thought. She yelled, "Let her go!"

The alien reached a console and punched a button on a panel. Luxmi heard a crackling sound from the cruiser's intercom and then the alien's voice:

"I want to live. Turn round."

"No," Davidos countered. "We go on."

'Might as well establish the boundaries!' she thought.

"Then I die. She dies. Maybe you all die. One shot and this cruiser can be disabled. Now I am here, it's easy." There followed a horrible sound, like a dog laughing.

"Then we all die; I don't care," Luxmi lied.

While the alien's eyes were fixed on the the new commander of the cruiser, Luxmi herself could see Baker slowly edging towards the Ischian from an angle which put her out of both alien's field of vision. Luxmi kept talking:

"Let's just negotiate. Maybe we can do something for you."

"What? Make an offer Earth female."

"We can give you a POD when we get to our destinati- …."

Baker dived at the Ischian. He slammed into the eight foot monster but his body just crumpled to the floor. The Ischian pulled the trigger. A brief burst of white light lit up the cabin and Pfenigshaven collapsed, a neat hole in both sides of her head.

Luxmi dived for the alien and she saw several more grunts try the same idea. The Ischian female spun and fired at Luxmi but the Major had already launched herself through air, head down. The shot seared through her black hair. The next instant, she slammed into the alien's chest. Another grunt had gone for the alien's legs and, together, they brought her down. She fired wildly but most of her shots only took out a few ceiling lights in the gangway.

The alien wasn't finished, however. She knew she fought for her life. She punched Luxmi in the face and managed to turn on to her front. This allowed her to get her legs underneath her. From there, she knelt knelt and opened fire. She would have seen the X.77 a moment before its red beam bored through her skull, shattering the back and mixing her brains into a goulash of greenish-grey meat. She fell forward, over Pfenigshaven's lifeless body.

Luxmi Davidos struggled to her feet. Everything spun inside her head. One of the grunts helped her to the nearest seat, in front of the remaining Ischian who still squatted, bound.

When Luxmi's vision cleared, she stared at the smaller alien. She noticed two unusual things about the Ischian; that blood spurted from between its claws from a wound probably inflicted by a stray shot from her leader and that one of its two boots lay on the floor. Luxmi stood unsteadily and told two grunts to turn the Ischian round.

The alien had six digits, both on fore and hind paws. Peering between the first and second digits of the alien's hairy, hind paw, Luxmi saw blood.

"Been busy have we?" she commented. "I didn't know Ischians had horizontally opposed thumbs on their rear paws as well! So that's how you untied the knots! Ha! You learn something every day!"

The alien seemed in great pain but managed a scowl and said, "You know nothing!" before passing out.

***

4 days until Zero Hour

I had been setting up a gas detector in J5's torus when my headband told me what I had been waiting to hear: a message had been received from somebody on the frequency of my transmission.

"Download," I said. But I couldn't understand the stream of gibberish that assailed my ears. "Sounds distinctly like Ischian to me! Oh shit!" I cut it off before ten seconds had passed.

Back in the POD, I played the whole message back through a translator. It did indeed begin with some kind of Ischian security warning, which sounded, at the same time, standard and inexplicable.

Have they found me?

I skipped forward about thirty seconds and cut in to the middle of a short message from a woman. "Rewind ten seconds." I said. I repeated in decreasing increments until I found the beginning of the message:

> "Eight survivors from S.4 leaving now. Estimate arrival: a little over three hours. Will signal name in your code. Do not defend."

I sat back in my chair like a man who has caught a big fish, but not a species he expected. The message dumfounded me.

Three hours? Alien transmission equipment? What's going on? And 'Do not defend;' What the hell am I supposed to do if I don't recognise you?

I hastily ate something and made preparations for ten new arrivals while muttering to myself. With nothing else to do, I returned to the field where I had been setting up the gas detector. I took a reading for the Oxygen: one part in one hundred thousand.

One thousandth of a percent! At this rate it won't be breathable for years!

I left the detector in place and considered what to do next about the signal.

Of course, it could be a trick. The Ischians may have detected me after all. Perhaps they don't know our strength: one!

I sat down on a tuft of weed at the side of the field. How does weed manage to find a foothold, even in genetically engineered wheat on a space station?

I had been thinking about defences for the Station but there seemed very little I could do on my own. The Station had a modest array of defensive missiles but those had all apparently been fired. There might be spares but they would be dangerous to handle now and the systems themselves were in-operative. Apart from a few laser cannons, the station seemed defenceless.

As I worked, planting more Hyper-Oxygen Producing plants, or HOPs, from the store, my mind turned again and again to the sight of Frisky's rigid body.

What had happened to him? My best guess is that my mother must have given him one quick, loving stab to his heart. A rule existed on J5 that; if one kept pets, one did so with the knowledge that there would be no space on the escape PODs for them. A quick death would have been the humane thing for him and Mary certainly was tough enough, and had the biological knowledge, to do it cleanly. She probably used a carving knife. I nodded to myself.

It would have broken her heart to do it.

And what did Kek mean when he said I would be meeting Stone again? Does he mean in some kind of heaven? Or the kind of spirit continuum, or river, that they talk about in the Blue Path?

I had still been considering this when a movement caught my eye. I glanced up. Through the transparent section of torus above me, I could see a yellow and black shape; an Ischian cruiser.

Oh no!

My heart thumped hard, twice before I relaxed.

Three hours, she said. It could be...

I hurried to the main Control Room. A big success of mine had been to make one of the transmitter/receiver arrays and its controls functional. There were two main arrays on J5. It looked as if relaxing Ischian cruiser crews had shot off the other one for target practice; there were burn marks on the stubs of gantries that remained. I switched the console to receive and heard a voice coming out of the speaker:

"Hello. J5. Are you receiving? S.4 survivors on board Ischian cruiser. We cannot see any alien craft. Can you confirm it's safe to dock? Over."

"J5 control here. Yes, I can confirm it's safe to dock. Go to rear Dock 18. I have prepared it for you. Nice to hear a voice up here! Especially human!"

"Roger that!"

The owner of the voice came out of the dock first; a very attractive young female soldier with unusual, lop-sided, dark hair. She stepped up to me and saluted. I thought she looked more surprised than me.

"Major Luxmi Davidos. Sir!"

With my suit on, I probably looked like I still served in the USAC. My non army-length hair might normally have given me away but the man behind her had a goatee. Times were changing.

"I'm not a serving officer anymore Major Davidos."

She smiled. "I recognised you from the files. Gen- … Mister Nanden. It's good to meet you. Can I shake your hand?"

"If you like." I detached my glove and took her small hand. She had a firm grip.

"Pleased to meet you, sir!" said the man behind her. "Lieutenant Deitner... USAC..." He grinned.

One by one, eight other men exited the cruiser wearily and introduced themselves. At the back, between two grunts with X.259s stood one, sorry looking, bandaged Ischian prisoner. I directed the two grunts to the brig, where the alien could be locked up.

"Are you *it*?" I asked the Major. "I mean; are there any others out there, do you think? USAC?"

"Not on the outer side of the Moon. I doubt it."

"Yeah the Moon has been nuked of course. Thank God; after most had got off!"

I gritted my teeth.

"Yeah. I have often wondered about that," said Davidos. "Wouldn't it have been useful to them?"

"They're only after iron," I replied. "Not much of it on the Moon."

"But there must be a thousand planets out there with plenty of iron. Why here?" asked Deitner.

"Yes. But those planets don't have millions, whom they can enslave as miners."

Everyone fell silent.

"How about Venus?" I asked.

"Well, there was still some fighting going on there, last I heard. And on that new J6. But that was weeks ago..."

"Right. Well follow me. I have your quarters all set up. It's in one of the escape PODS; very comfortable."

"Wait. I forgot my grubber!" Davidos ran back into the cruiser and returned, carrying a box. Something scratched restlessly inside.

"Grubber?" I asked.

"Explain later."

Within fifteen minutes, they were showering and fixing themselves coffee.

I could see they were all exhausted so I set a conference, or 'briefing,' as Deitner insisted on calling it, for the following day at noon, Lunar Time. I showed them their bunks and then went back to my own tasks.

I soon found myself back inside the torus' inner space, planting more seeds. Luxmi's answer to my question about survivors in the Solar System devastated me. I had tried not to show it.

All of them... from J5. Just gone! Vanished! But then maybe it's always like this at moments when history is made; when things change and there is great loss. The details are lost...

Somebody tapped me on the shoulder, startling me. I swung round sharply, raising the hoe.

"Sorry. Couldn't sleep." Luxmi stood beside me. I couldn't see her face through the suit visor, because it had darkened to combat the bright sunlight in the torus, but I recognised her voice on the intercom.

"How did you find me?"

"Station schematics were all over your desk. There seemed to be a lot of focus on this area. I can see you are really at home here. You had relatives here didn't you?"

"My mother, sister... and a dog, Frisky."

"Okay..."

"Surprised I mention a dog? There's a bit of a mystery around his death. I found his body... with a knife wound. I have been trying to figure out what happened..."

"I'm sorry."

"We've all lost people..."

"Yes. Although with me, it's just a useless layabout boyfriend... who worked in a pie shop!"

"Ha! Ha!" I looked into her eyes but she looked deadly serious.

"Yes. I am."

"And the others?" I asked.

"All 'R-Company.' That makes you the only full-human here."

"I hate that term, 'full-human,'" I said, too hastily. "I thought I was a replicant too, once…"

"I know. I read your history." She seemed to look for somewhere to put her hands but space-suits don't have pockets. "God! I never felt like this before!"

"Like what?"

"Feeling sorry for someone 'cause they're *not* a repo!"

"Hm. I'll live! I've been alienated before!" I said brightly. We both broke into laughter at the inappropriateness of my remark. "I notice you say 'history' and not 'biography.' I *am* history."

"Not yet, you're not."

That silenced me. It had been a while since I had felt admired by a pretty, young woman. There followed a very long pause, during which time I continued to turn the Nitrogen-rich soil with my hoe. She followed me.

"How do they grow?" she asked.

"Variation on photosynthesis. They are a genetically-engineered adaptation from Ischian plants. Like many other things now."

"Like Digby."

"Who?"

"My grubber. I decided to call him Digby. He's genetically-engineered to clean out fuel lines and recycling lines. I think S.4 was the first to get them. It's like a giant worm. That's why I called him Digby. I think he would be happy digging around in your soil."

"Hm. Well anyway, the plants... They don't need Oxygen. They take the Nitrogen from the soil and, with a few catalysts, in their internal structure, they *produce* Oxygen … as well as being quite tasty. The wheat is particularly good but I've run out!"

"But they need water?"

"Not much. There is enough in the soil, for now. Besides, there are water tanks on board. We have enough, for now. Eventually, they will start producing condensation; clouds."

"Wow! I heard that... that you get clouds in here. I've never seen clouds."

We were both silent again but this time it felt like a comfortable silence.

"Nice hair," I said.

She grinned. "Lucky Ischian laser shot."

I grinned. "One thing I'm dying to know … ." I continued.

"Yes?"

"Did you really get here in three hours?"

"Not much *more*."

"So how does it work then? This drive. It's the Pulse Drive, isn't it?"

"Mm hm. I translated the ship's manual. There is a condensed explanation in there. My translator didn't like the technical words. It's amazing though! They are clever bastards, I'll give 'em that!"

"Well?"

"You want the condensed version?"

"Please."

"Okay. It's used on cruisers to generate speeds up to point five times the speed of light: it uses pulses of energy from one-atom sized singularities to generate a gravity gradient which the ship can ride... rather like getting a sling-shot around a star. This is done by using a quantum-photon multiplier, which falsely duplicates photon-encrypted data and this is sent back to two detectors, which initially generate the quanta, surrounding one atom each of a heavy element, often lead. These are 'fooled' into detecting atoms with electrons in every conceivable location in the atoms' inner orbits. Because of the peculiarity in quantum behaviour that the 'detector effects the detected', the electrons 'believe' they already occupy the lower orbits and thus move … or gravitate … Ha! Ha! … to ever higher and higher orbits … erm … making the element behave like an impossibly heavy one for the duration of the pulse, and thus generating a singularity. This is inherently unstable and if the pulse is too long, the ship will … erm … disappear into a black hole of its own making. So the pulse is switched from matter to anti-matter like AC/DC current to even out the pulse's effect. It's a simple, but very effective system."

"Yeah! I can see you're not sleepy! Wow! That's a really cool system. And a cool bit of science. Come on, I've done enough hoeing. Let's get something to eat."

There were eleven of us sitting in the gangway of the escape POD the next day for the conference. I opened the discussion as chair by first clarifying the aim of the meeting; to decide on some kind of retaliation against the Ischians. Then I motioned for us to assess the situation so far. I told them about my faith, the Blue Path, and my strange connectivity, for want of a better word, with my Ischian friend Kek-suîxjh. I concluded by telling them what Kek-suîxjh had told me about the strengths and weaknesses of the space-battleship and its Commander. Ten stunned faces stared at me.

After a brief pause, Luxmi cleared her throat. "Well, if there was any doubt before who should lead us, I think that particular detail is cleared up now!" She glanced up and down the corridor and saw a lot of nodding heads.

"Well, a week ago, I wouldn't have been interested," I said. "But I heard of the death of my second … my last … son a few days ago. Now, I am set on doing whatever it takes to get these … bastards off our planet … I am going down fighting and if anybody wants to come along, they would be most welcome!"

"But what can we actually do?" cut in Deitner. "I mean, practically? There are just eleven of us."

"And J5," I replied.

"And an Ischian cruiser," added Luxmi. "At the very least, and as a last resort, we could ram that dirty great fucker over the pole."

"Yeah … I thought of that," I said. "But only as a last resort. Of course if we *could* … ram it with J5, we would smash it to pieces but we would never get close enough." There were some quizzical looks in the gangway. "Oh yes! J5 can move, alright. Some of you may not know this but the J Stations were originally designed by NASA, way back in the 20th Century, as kind of lifeboats, if humans destroyed Earth's atmosphere in warfare. It looks like it will be *someone else* who does this now. It's worth you knowing this; J5 has thousands of tiny hydrogen thrusters around the rim of the torus, in two rows. It is possible to direct these to accelerate the Station in any one direction. It would take a *long time* to get there but it *could*, in theory, reach speeds of up to 28,000 miles per hour. Nobody's ever tried it. You may have to try this one day. That's why I'm telling you."

"That might be our best bet. Running, I mean," interjected one of the grunts "It seems to me we don't have a chance … ." Luxmi and Deitner shook their heads.

"No. There's always a chance," I replied, remembering a lecture at the Academy. "Napoleon left the island of Elba on his own but reached Paris with a whole army! All you need is self-belief!"

"And a bloody good reputation for leadership and tactics!" added Luxmi.

"Who is *Napoleon*?" asked Deitner.

"He was a Corporal, then a General and finally Emperor of France... a long time ago," I replied. "And there is the Trojan horse. Hm … ." I nodded to myself. Luxmi gave me a curious look.

She pulled a loose thread on her trousers. "I think the cruiser offers us the best chance," she offered. "As Mister Nanden has said, the battleship will b-… ."

"Please, call me Jake. Humour me. It makes me feel much younger."

Luxmi continued, "… as Jake has said, the battleship already at the North Pole will be joined by another any day now. Our best chance is to destroy, or even take, if possible, the battleship and turn it against our enemy. While there's still time. If we could pose as Ischians and get on board the battleship … ." She left the enticing thought hanging in the air.

"Exactly," I added. "A Trojan horse. If we can get inside, then we have a chance; a very good chance. If we can control that ship, we control the board, as the chess term goes. The alien commander is like the Queen, in a game of chess."

"Yes sir. I agree with all that," responded Deitner. "But then they have hundreds, perhaps thousands, of cruisers. Against those, we will struggle … I think we'll be overwhelmed … ."

"Hm. Perhaps you're right," I replied. "I am betting you they designed this ship to be resistant to attacks by ships equal in destructive force to their own cruisers. It's a familiar planner's tactic and mistake; to use your own attacking forces as models for the enemy. But as for the numbers they have … . Does anybody know how many cruisers they actually have?"

For a moment, I heard only silence.

"Last I heard," Luxmi said, quietly, "in a transmission from Mars, the estimate was four hundred to eight hundred,"

"That sounds too high to me," I replied. "Probably natural really. Sort of, hysterical estimate based on fear. I will see if I can find out from my Ischian friends what the real figure is. I think we could take out two hundred, at most..."

"Even if it *is* four hundred and we take out two hundred … ," said Deitner, sounding more exasperated, "… we still have a big problem. Don't you see? Manpower! Even if we can overcome the battleship, *and* can somehow subdue or take out two hundred of these things, we don't have the manpower to crew them, if we want to fight their whole fleet! I bet they haven't sent their whole navy. And you said there are more battleships to come..! And there is the army on Mars... and probably on Earth, by now."

I looked at him, shaken by this new revelation. "Army? On Mars? I didn't..."

"Yes! They have incarcerated the whole population, and as far as I know, enslaved, somehow, all four USAC battalions based there!"

"But I haven't heard this?" cut in Luxmi. "When did you hear this?"

"About a week ago. It was a weak signal, coming for Mars. At first we thought it was a trick but it *wasn't*. We talked to them!"

"So they have how many troops there, do you think?" I queried.

"Well, their guess was two thousand. I would put it a bit higher, probably four thousand. If I were the Ischians, and I had the *forces* they have, I would want to be on the safe side."

"What do you mean; forces they have?" I asked. Something in his tone made me think he knew something else I didn't.

"They have a whole huge army of these Bekians, a smaller race, some say genetically-engineered from a colony on a planet called Bek-su. I have seen … . we have *all* seen two of *them*." He looked at Luxmi. "Our two captives were Bekians."

"But I just thought they were small … ." she began.

I cut in. "Wait. I do remember something about this. Long ago. My son, Stone, told me about them. I'd forgotten; bad mistake. One of my Ischian friends estimated there was an adult male population of perhaps one million there. If only half of those is fit for active service … ." I felt shaken. Everyone else fell silent. Finally I gathered myself to speak:

"It seems we will not come up with a plan today," I interjected. "However, we don't have much time. The second Ischian battleship will be here any moment. It's not the end, but it will get harder. We'll meet again tomorrow at noon, and the next day, if necessary. But by then, we *must* have a plan, however desperate."

***

Chapter Five

3 days until Zero Hour

"No! No! No!"

I woke up sweating; the sweat of conflicted thought, of a body trying to contain a mind that would not rest. I clambered out of my bunk and poured a cup of cold water.

Somebody had been yelling, "No! No! No!"

It must have been me!

I sat back on the bunk but I didn't feel like sleeping. The phrase 'Iron in the Soul' kept going through my head. Stone often used to talk about this after his little trip to ancient Earth. Right now, I felt that I didn't have *any* iron in *my* soul! I felt *uncommitted* to the Blue Path, slowly relinquishing all my beliefs to a desire for revenge. I had lived almost the whole of my adult life with this one aim; revenge. It seemed to me that the Blue Path's main teaching had been one of determinism. But I felt the cool current of fatalism start to flow in *my* soul. Yes, I *had* once been fatalistic. Now it seemed I wanted to be *so* again. It gave me a sense of peace I had missed without realising it.

But this is against the Blue Path!

"Not necessarily," a little voice inside my head seemed to say. I wondered if Kek had something to do with this.

Yes! Perhaps fatalism is a kind of commitment; a kind of faith in itself. Very well. I embrace my old fatalism.

What will be, will be. I will beat the Ischians or die trying!

I felt peaceful at once and lay down, hoping to find sleep. It took me, at last.

When I rose, I organised a game of five-aside soccer. We used to play it in my MSC on Io and I thought it would improve morale. The two teams of five, led by Luxmi and Hani Deitner, played on one of J5's many pitches wearing full spacesuits. I took the role of referee. The temperature inside the torus remained steady at twelve degrees Centigrade but both teams were sweating after ten minutes. I saw a good deal of aggression and a lot of laughter during those ninety minutes. Deitner's team won by twelve goals to eleven. Both goalies left a lot to be desired. After we all showered, I checked the radio for any incoming transmissions. I needed something to make the plan in my head work. I listened to one, short, gut-wrenching message from Muna:

> Bad news: the second alien battleship has
> been seen approaching the South Pole. Will be
> in place within 24 hours.

I relayed the information to everyone else as I returned to my bunk. Emotions dropped to their lowest point. Everyone fell silent.

That day, however, would be one of extreme highs and lows. I tried to grab some sleep.

***

3 days until Zero Hour

I woke up with an idea. At first, it didn't seem a good one, almost a flight of fantasy, but as the second conference approached, I became resolved to air it.

"Where's Major Davidos," I asked.

"Not sure sir. She said she had to go to the cruiser," replied Sergeant Baker.

Ten minutes later, and only five minutes before the conference was due to start, the reason for her absence became clear. She ran up to me, out of breath and looking very stern:

"Downloaded a message … . Set my headband to alert me to any... thing incoming... Cruiser radio tuned to USAC frequency. I have to tell you... two Ischian cruisers heading this way... from Venus! Only survivors, both have almost four hundred men on board … survivors from two battalions … . Told them to come … here!"

Her expression changed to one of joy and the corridor erupted in laughter, shouts of. "Hooray!" and applause.

"Be here in four hours … . *if* they make it!" she added.

I wacked the wall with glee but a little voice screamed something inside me. I tried to disconnect from the party atmosphere for a moment. "Wait!" I shouted, seeing it finally. "We have to tell them to zigzag! If they come straight here, the Dogs will be on to us!" I, too, now used the term 'Dog.'

"Thought of that. Told them to go past, double back and approach from the far side to Earth. Should be okay," Luxmi added.

Clever girl!

"In that case, I suggest we delay the meeting... at least until this evening," I suggested. There were only lots of nodding heads in response. This changed everything. "Major Davidos. Come with me!"

"Where are we going?" she asked as we suited up.

"We can't accommodate eight hundred men in the POD! But I have an idea. The old maintenance block, used as accommodation while the station was being built, is capable of isolated pressurisation. Now it's used just for storage, or was, but if we can re-pressurise it and clear it out..."

"*With* you! Can we do it in time?"

"We have to!"

We began by locating the main air-lock to the section and restoring its functionality. Consisting of two doors, it had been welded open to admit the frequent entrance of Ford Forkos; the modern fork-elevator equivalent of hoovers in ubiquity. One by one, we checked all the air-lock doors and the general structure. Then we checked the ducting and pumps. The pumps were in a sorry state; untended and some missing for many years. While I worked on restarting some of them, Luxmi tried to figure out how to transfer recycled air from all three cruisers to the maintenance storage tanks; since these were part of the main storage tank network, it seemed highly likely the tanks would still be in good working order. She returned within thirty minutes.

"Any luck?" she asked, over the intercom.

"Two, so far. We need at least *five*. How about you?"

"Well, we need at least five hundred meters of ducting, say about three to six inches diameter, to get it to the nearest insertion point. That is, unless you know the Station's own systems well enough to direct it correctly through the system? Lucky we're not further from the cruisers."

"I could show you the system and let *you* work it out? But I think it's too dangerous. If we get it wrong, we will lose the air for good inside this place. I know where there's ducting. Don't forget though, we will need to get it back into the cruisers when we've finished."

"Is it worth it for just a few days? We don't have any longer, as you *say*."

"Are you joking? They must be packed like sardines in there! By the time they get here, they will be close to asphyxiation!"

"You're right."

"Besides. I have been generating some clean air here – on the Station. I can redirect *that*…"

"Oh no! Not your precious *air*!"

"Yes! It hurts." We smiled at my irony. Another awkward silence followed.

"Well, I better get on it," Luxmi said. "Show me the ducting. I'll get a couple of the grunts to help." I had still been working hard on the fifth generator two hours later when she returned. "All patched in and ready to go," she announced.

"Just a minute … ," I replied. "Stuck valve. Had to take the head off and clean it out. Good job somebody is old enough to remember how these things work!" I gasped as my arm reached around a bend behind the motor to tighten a bolt. "Just a few more minutes..."

"I'll wait."

At last, I felt ready to try the intransigent motor. I checked the clutch had been pulled in and pressed the manual starter button. The corridor lights blinked for moment as the large motor drained the station's electrical power. It made a horrible scuffing noise and then seemed to gain momentum. Before long, it sang away, at full power. "Okay. Let's try the whole thing." I switched in the clutch, the flywheel disengaged and the fan blades in the circular-section duct started to turn. I ran to the other motors and started each in turn. "All sucking," I shouted. "Tell them to start pumping it out!" She spoke into her helmet mike and then followed me back into the nearest maintenance compartment. It had two bunks, both folded against the wall. Crates, piled high, still filled the room.

I took a deep breath and started moving the crates out into the corridor. When I had cleared it, I folded out a bunk and collapsed onto it. "I'm knackered! Too old for this..."

Luxmi came and sat on the edge of the bunk. "It's not just age! I need a *holiday* ... . How much air you got left?"

"Fifteen minutes. You?"

"Twenty-five."

"We better get going."

"Why? If we close the doors ... ."

"Yes?"

"We can try it out. Should only take a few minutes." She sealed both doors to the compartment and sat back down on the bunk. She rested against my legs. I didn't move them. "I'll go first." She waited thirty seconds and then released her helmet. Shaking her hair loose, she grinned and took her first breath, cautiously. "It's fine!"

I released my helmet and breathed in the air. "Wow!"

"Isn't it *great*? J5 is coming alive!"

"Yeah!"

"Now, let's get these suits off!"

"Why? We need them to get back."

"Yeah but we don't need them now. We only have a few minutes to try what it feels like to be free of a suit on J5. Besides, it might be the last chance I get to dress normally outside some cramped POD or cruiser! Come on, it will be a laugh!"

I complied, slowly. My whole body ached. "We can't stay long..." Luxmi's forthright nature made me nervous.

"Shy, are we? That's good. Modest as well as deep. I like modesty in a man." She had already removed her suit and proceeded to remove her T-shirt. She had no bra on. She turned her back to me but even her naked back turned me on. Then she turned to face me with her arms crossed over her breasts.

"You are … ."

"Yes? I am … ?" She walked over and sat with her back to me on the bunk.

I took a deep breath. "Beautiful!"

"Am I?" She sat completely still for a moment and then suddenly stood and removed her combat trousers. She wore nothing underneath and now stood completely naked. I hurriedly removed my shirt but then froze. She suddenly turned and lay beside me, pressing herself into my chest, nestling her head under my chin. I wanted to envelop her with my arms but they wouldn't move. "Don't," she whispered.

"Don't?"

"Don't resist. Things are bad. This might be the last chance I... we, get! We haven't got time for your shyness... or mine!" Her body pressed against me like a survivor. I felt her need for comfort, for affection. I put my arms around her and kissed the silky black hair on top of her head. She felt so warm, so alive. She seemed to be wriggling to get even closer to me. I placed my hand tentatively on her ass and she sighed.

I already felt my hardness. She could feel it. She started to undo my trousers. I let her. When my pants were removed, she kissed my erection and put her mouth around it. I threw my wrist over my eyes; a gesture many use and I have never understood the meaning of.

"Stop!" I said.

I lifted her head gently away from my groin and eased her over onto her back beside me. I stared for a moment at the beauty of her whole body. She smiled and I smiled back. I put my face between her thighs and began to lick her. Exploring with my tongue, felt for those tiny rhythms in her muscles that indicate pleasure. At first, she seemed nervous and her body a little stiff. But she reached down, stroked the stop of my balding head and relaxed. Together, we explored each other's rhythms; mine a little more aggressive, hers very sensitive and responsive. As always with a woman, I felt tentative about pushing her too hard, too fast. With my fingers, I cupped her breasts and caressed her nipples. She whispered something.

"What?" I asked.

"They're sensitive. Don't stop." I felt that the time to be right. I moved up to face her and while we stared into each other's eyes, I entered her. "Oh yes! Jake!"

"Luxmi," I whispered. My thighs felt hard as iron as I finally climaxed inside her. She smiled at me. "You didn't … ," I began to say. For fear I would fall asleep if I waited, I began licking her again. It wasn't long before she writhed in ecstasy. Finally, she shuddered and pulled at my arms. I moved up beside her, cradling her shoulders in my arms. We lay silently. We didn't utter a single word for only a few minutes but it seemed like a lifetime.

"We better go," she said simply. We put on our suits, exited the air-lock and started towards the POD.

***

3 days until Zero Hour

"They're here!" came the message over both our headbands. Luxmi and I detoured from the maintenance block to the docking area. The red lights were flashing on Dock 13 and 16. We took a dock each, just in time to see the two companies of very weary men and women, exit, and direct them to their new quarters.

"There's air there, now. You're in the old maintenance block," I explained to their leader, a Lieutenant Colonel Mayer, "But we only just got the air-supply working. Your men will have to clean out all the crates. Tell them to pile them, intact, outside the block. We may need the stuff later. Sorry. I know your men are tired but … ."

"No problem … er … . Mister?"

"Nanden. Jake Nanden."

"Oh. Oh, I see. Well … . General Nanden, sir, we can take care of it. Food and water?"

"Just Mister Nanden. I'm no longer active. Yes. We have plenty of n-gens on board. I will have some installed in the next few hours. However, there is just one thing … ."

"*Yes*. There's something I have to tell you too. The … Dogs, as you guys are calling them, will soon figure out where we are. They'll be here within forty-eight hours, at most." He looked as if he would normally be chomping a cigar, if he could get one. His jaw set like a bunker wall and his steely blue eyes, set beneath a shot crop of salt and pepper hair, looked like they had modelled for a recruitment poster. He looked like the archetypal USAC Colonel.

"Oh. Yes. I guess you're right. Well that is just what I was going to say anyway. We had a conferences already; we seem to be the only free … resistance left in the Solar system and we need to decide what to do before tomorrow. As you say, there is very little time. When can you and the other battalion commander be ready for a conference?"

"Well … apart from a stinking headache from those damned light levels on the cruiser – we downloaded part of the manual before shootin' but USAC transmissions cut out completely before we got the bit about turning down the light levels. Shoot us full of coffee and we'll be ready in half an hour. If you have a cigar … that would be even better!" I laughed and he grinned back. "But you know … ." he continued. "We're not the last. An old freighter radioed us about half hour ago. I recognise the ship; it's an old Rebel light freighter called The Cleopatra. It's very fast and the captain is one of the best I ever came across. He could fly the thing through the eye of a needle. He's been doing the run from Earth to Mars for the last twenty years. I know the Ischians are after him. He's out there somewhere and if anyone can get here, he will."

"How many men?"

"Oh … only about a dozen, I guess. But they'll be useful."

"Okay. Not a problem. Let's hope they get here in time for the … may as well call it a 'summit.'"

***

3 days until Zero Hour

I called for the summit in one hour but delayed again because of The Cleopatra's arrival. She looked a pretty sorry sight. Coming in on one engine, and with holes you could ride a hoverbike through, she took a great deal of effort, and some assistance from the POD, to dock. Its weary crew of outcast replicants were shown to their quarters and I had the Captain, Dragodes, brought to the summit. We had moved this to one of the large storage rooms in the maintenance section. While most of the new arrivals slept, two of the men who had arrived with Luxmi manned the Control Room, watching for intruders. The assembled leaders occupied the front seats, with Colonel Mayer smoking the huge cigar we had conjured up from an n-gen. In front of them, we had projected a hologram of the Solar System on which we had plotted, to the best of our ability, the Ischian forces and remaining USAC forces. Prominent on the image were the two giant Ischian battleships, poised over each pole of Earth.

At the last moment, Luxmi had introduced me to the tall, black Major, Osei, and I had the chance to ask him the question that had been burning in my mind since she had been told me his name. I stood facing the muscular man, who grinned, exposing a healthy set of fine teeth. He had a small tattoo of a dagger under his left ear, a silver stud in the ear and a shaven head.

"Are you related to Ricky Osei?" I asked.

"Sure. He was my older brother. And I know who *you* are sir! I have been dying to meet you."

"He was a good man, a very good man."

"Yeah. He thought highly of you. You saw him go down, in the mine. Or at least that's what I've been told. Is it true? You know they often make these things up, to make us feel good."

"Yes. I was there. I saw him get hit. He died instantly. He didn't suffer."

"Thanks. I guess we better get on with it."

I looked up and the whole room seemed to be waiting for me.

"Well. I guess I better chair this... Summit, dammit!" I began. "First of all, I have been thinking…" I stared at my feet as I took the floor, just a space cleared in front of the two rows of chairs. My head swam between the planets of the Solar System in the hologram. "Officially I am not an active member of USAC. I retired long ago but, since I seem to be the most senior non-active officer left to fight these bastards, I am hereby reactivating my service. So from now on, you may call me General Nanden!" A huge eruption of applause met my announcement. "Thanks. Now, down to business."

I reiterated what we knew so far of the Ischian forces and our own, for the benefit of the newcomers, and concluded briefly with my own connections to the Ischian Rebel faction. I had to wave down a few raised hands and silence a persistent hum at this point but I pushed on. Then, I asked the two newly arrived commanding officers and Captain Dragodes to add anything new they could contribute to this. Colonel Mayer, a tall, muscular man, stood up:

"It's true that the Dogs have subdued Mars, and your information is consistent with ours; that includes four full battalions of troops and their equipment. My guess is that it's probably mostly these smaller Dogs, Bekians, as you call them, that are there. With a few of the bigger ones, of course, to command them. Where the rest of them are, who knows? I have something else I have to tell you. And it's not pleasant, I'm afraid. A few days ago, the remaining populations on Venus were nuked. That's after they nuked J6. That means, unless there are survivors on the scientific station around Mercury, we really are the only free forces still operating."

There were gasps around the room. After a pause, I nodded to Osei. He didn't have anything to add to this.

Captain Dragodes had incongruously black hair for the craggy face it framed, and a thick black beard. "I can only confirm what Colonel Mayer has said," he added with a droll, acerbic tone. He coughed twice as if to punctuate his reply.

Bad smoker.

"Right," I said. "I think we have all the facts that we're going to get at our disposal!" "We now have to decide what to do. Does anybody have any ideas?" My question met with silence and slowly shaking heads. "Well, yesterday we proposed taking one of the Ischian battleships, possibly using a cruiser posing as one of their own, possibly even by ramming, and then using this as the leverage to start a fight back. With just one of those ships, we reckoned we can take out perhaps one hundred or two hundred Ischian ships. Better still to take them intact. But then we have the problem of manpower. I am still hoping to find out exactly how many ships they have in our system; estimates vary from four hundred to a thousand. Let's take the average for now: seven hundred. If we can capture two hundred and we have the two battleships, using the first to take the second, perhaps – just perhaps – we have a chance. As I said, manpower is the issue. Major Davidos, you know these Ischian cruisers well; what is the minimum crew they need?"

"Well, the one that took S.4 had a crew of about thirty-five. Given the *size* of the controls and the complexity, fifty would be my minimum estimate. You will probably need four just to keep reading the manual I have dug up!" Laughter bubbled up around the room.

"Right. That means we need five thousand of us just to fly one hundred of those ships. And that's not including the battleships. *My* guess is, by the way, that the rest of the Bekians are on the two battleships, ready to be sent down to Earth as slave-masters. We were already seeing this kind of behaviour in Washington, where I was trapped until recently. Their natural instinct is to dominate and enslave. Does anybody have any suggestion for the manpower problem?" There were no offers. "Well I *do*. The colony on Mars. It occurred to me this morning; the reason the Ischians have nuked Venus, J6 and the Moon is because those are not rich in iron. This is what they're after. But Mars *is*. That is why they're there in force. But it may be the weak link in their chain. Iron is hard to mine on Mars; the ore itself is deep down, and mostly in dispersed seams. The stuff on the surface is just the oxide. This means they will need a lot of manpower, or slaves, to mine it. These will mainly be USAC. Earth will be almost as tough to mine, but there, they will be able to use mostly civilians. Those two places are where their strength will be focused. As you know, this morning, a second battleship took up position over the South Pole. They will very soon, in the next few hours at most, have Earth in the grip of a huge defensive field. It will keep us out, and the rest of Earth's population in. I can tell you that I know six more ships will arrive, probably sometime in the next twelve months. Things will get a lot worse then. We have to act now. Furthermore, Colonel Mayer estimates the … Dogs will be onto us already. They will be here, at J5, within the next forty-eight hours at most. We need a plan tonight and after a final briefing tomorrow, we must act. Any questions?"

"Yes. One," said Captain Dragodes. "How reliable are these friends of yours. Frankly, I haven't met an Ischian yet that *I* actually liked; good to do business with but I don't trust 'em."

Applause and laughter rippled around the room.

"Let's just say; one of them communicates with me in my sleep, has done since my days in USAC. I have never found his advice or information to be faulty. Right. I propose we take the Ischian battleship using two cruisers as Trojan-horses. If we all pack in, we may just be able to take the ship. I know its weaknesses and I will brief you in detail on this in just a moment. Now, things will move very fast once this happens. We won't have time to plan a Phase Two. Therefore, I also propose that Captain Dragodes take his ship, if it can be repaired, to Mars to start a rebellion there or at least warn the USAC forces there what we're up to. If anybody can get through, Colonel Mayer assures me, Captain Dragodes can. Simultaneously, the third cruiser *must* get through to Earth. There are already enough Ischians on Earth to give them a firm power base. If we don't free the populations of Washington and Los Angeles, so that they can unite forces on Earth, I believe we will ultimately face defeat anyway. At the very least, the Dogs will hold us to ransom with them. We do have some free allies on Earth. I have personally met with Muna, the Desert Princess or The Princess as some call her. She has a large force of Rebels at her disposal and we'll need to liaise with her too."

I saw nods of approval, so I continued:

"Now, the key to this whole operation is getting inside the Ischian battleship. They're not going to just let us in. And even if they do, these ships are vastly complex and difficult to run. We cannot risk an all-out gun-fight; we'll just blow ourselves up. What we need to do is control the head of the snake; the Commander. I know a little about her, again from our Ischian Rebel friends. She's tough, resourceful and ruthless. She is, in effect, the most senior operational officer in the Ischian Imperial Fleet. Does anybody have any ideas how we could do this?" All the faces in front of me were blank. I had hoped they wouldn't be. "Well. I have spoken enough. I propose we break for some food and a two hour workshop. Split into groups with Luxmi, Hani, Colonel Mayer, Captain Dragodes, Major Osei and myself as team-leaders, and try to work though all these problems. I will hand out plastics, breaking down the tasks."

In truth, I prayed somebody would come up with something because I had an idea already. And I didn't like it.

At the end of the two hours, however, apart from some good ideas on later parts of the plan, nobody had come up with anything to save me. There were various ideas for capturing, or 'turning,' the battleship's Commander, including bribery, hypnotism using a video link and even seduction, but none were likely to succeed. I took the floor again.

"Right. Thanks for all your suggestions. There is some good stuff there. So nobody has any ideas about taking this Commander Anchiabakii, or whatever her name is? I was afraid of that. Well I *do* have an idea. I wish to God that I didn't." I cleared my throat. "I'm glad one group came up with the idea of seduction. That's exactly what I propose to do, in a way. But not by conventional means. Some of you will have used blankers. All of you will know what they are. I've used them myself from time to time. Now I propose to use the idea to create a Trojan horse within a Trojan horse. I can tell you that Commander Anchiabakii is a notorious sexual experimenter. I am sure she will already have heard of the concept of blankers. It would allow her to experience sex with humans, both sexes, without actually having to take the risk of being present. If she hasn't thought of it already – and I'm betting she is already trying it – I propose to put the idea there. Subtly of course. Subtlety will be the name of the game here."

I am beginning to talk like a theologian, or a politician!

"Anyway... uh hm... we are gonna sell her a Mickey Finn. For the benefit of those unfamiliar with the term, it's something that knocks somebody out; renders them incapable. The drug in question is called Dihydroxycuinozone. It's an exotic hydrocarbon which excites certain synapses in the brain while muting almost all other brain activity; rather like some types of alcohol. The beauty of this stuff is that it can be tuned. One variant induces a coma-like state in the viewer, in which they can received and experience transmitted events as if they are actually happening to them. The other variant suppresses all upper-brain functionality around sensual perception while retaining basic motor-control and lower brain functions. With the exception that high states of adrenaline in the blanker will cause higher-brain functions to cut in. This is to guard against actual death or extreme danger events to the blanker who is usually, but not always, a replicant."

"We are going to persuade – induce is a better word – Anchiabakii to take a large dose of our Mickey Finn; enough to knock her out. At the same time, we're gonna launch an attack … ." A hand shot up. "Yes … Sergeant Baker, isn't it?"

"Yes. Why not simply give her enough to kill her, if that's possible?"

"I was coming to that. Actually, in large doses it will cause irreparable damage to the brain. In effect, the higher functions may not restart and lower functions will not restart properly; sort of brain-death. But killing her is not what we want."

"We don't?" Baker responded.

"No. Her death, serious as it would be to the Ischian Imperial Fleet, would simply result in her replacement … immediately. What we want is a power-vacuum. If she's unconscious, the command structure will break down. As I understand it, most of her subordinates are probably terrified of her. They will not want to act without her direct orders. This will give us a small window of opportunity."

"I assume you're going to stage some kind of sexual entertainment for her," Colonel Mayer began. "But won't you need two willing victims for this?"

"Yes. Exactly. We cannot guarantee she will stay under... and passive, *unless* she has something to occupy her. We're gonna have to guess the dose because, of course, Ischians are much larger than us. And she is probably particularly a very large Ischian. Females are usually bigger than males. So … yes we need two volunteers. And I will be one of them." I felt a jolt of revulsion as I said this.

From the audience, there came only stunned silence or raised eyebrows at first. Then I heard a rising undercurrent of murmurs which, distracted me. I tried to quell it:

"Please. I *have* thought about this. She already knows my name. Her career has been blighted by my son, Stone. Hers was the ship which fought his, and let it escape when he came back through the worm-hole. I'm quite sure the thought of having vicarious sex either with, or using the body of, Stone's father would dramatically increase the likelihood of her using the drug." There were a few nods or approval and the murmuring subsided. "So, let me continue – with my idea. Now, if we give her too much of the drug and it permanently incapacitates her, even better. Where I am not sure about this plan is whether we should try and get the two volunteers actually on board that battleship, the Luckshia I think it's called, or whether we can do this remotely. On board is preferable but I guess this is down to how safe we can make her feel. Both are options. I guess that's about it. Any questions?"

Two hands shot up.

"Yes, Major Osei?"

"This sounds fuckin' risky! How the hell are we gonna get her to take the bait?"

"Yes. Good question. I know somebody who is involved in the blanker trade on Earth... Oh yes, it still exists, and on Earth as well now. Apparently, there is a market for it. I'm sure the Ischians must already be getting involved. With a word in the right place..." I didn't tell them that by friend, I meant DeTunne, a drunk was currently seemed 'inoperative.' "Yes, Colonel Mayer?"

"At first, I didn't like the idea. I don't like putting all our lives, and the possibility of salvation, on the line for such a dumb idea. But I really can't think of anything better! It's so crackpot, it just might work, sir, but how the devil are you... we going to coordinate all this?"

"Salvation is indeed the name of the game here and I'm glad you mentioned it."

I wasn't good at speaking and had been struggling for a word to encapsulate our aims and aspirations. 'Salvation' seemed to do it.

"I intend, if we agree this is the best plan, to assign each of you to detail, prepare and execute each part of the plan. Of course, once we start, communication might be difficult, or in some cases impossible. Some of you will need to get inside the domes on Earth, for instance. After that, it may well be every man for himself. If this works, gentlemen, and gentlewomen, we will have Global War. I don't like to say this but that is what is likely. I don't think this can be done cleanly. At least I can't think of a way, so all-out war is probably the only way we can hope to win. But I hope we can win. At the moment we're on the floor; almost knocked out. We have to stand up and fight!"

This met with a round of loud applause. Dragodes remained resolutely motionless.

"Fighting talk! That's what I like," Mayer said to Luxmi, sitting next to him. I noted that she had remained curiously silent throughout.

"I don't like it!" Dragodes said.

I knew what he said because I had been watching his mouth.

"Captain Dragodes?" I prompted.

The audience fell silent.

"It's a crazy plan. Most likely she will eat you for breakfast, figuratively speaking of course!"

"Yes. It's crazy," I replied. "But that might be its strength. Do you have anything better?"

He shook his head.

"Do you think you can have anything better before tomorrow?" I asked

He smiled and said, "I don't know."

"In that case, please, do all of you try and think of a better plan but we need time to prepare for a final briefing tomorrow at noon, Station time. That's in roughly fourteen hours. So I am going to have to put a deadline of four hours from now for any other ideas. That's 2 am. If you have one, please come and see me, or if I am asleep, let Luxmi or Hani, here know."

"The last thing to say is that Hani found a storage area chock-full of beer crates, full ones, a few hours ago. They must be sound because they survived the depressurisation. So in one hour, we will be serving beer to all and sundry in one of the rooms of the maintenance section. Let's make the most of one last party. I think we all need a little R and R."

This seemed to meet with little reaction. When I looked around my audience, I knew that I had never seen a more downcast bunch of faces. They were putting on a brave front but the mood in the room felt oppressive, like a morgue. It would take some doing to motivate them.

Passing between the rows of seats, towards the door, I grabbed the sleeve of Hani and Luxmi, and called Dragodes over.

"Both of you. I want you to help Captain Dragodes repair his ship in record time. Captain, what do you need?"

"Well. The engine is … gone! Shot off! I need a new engine. Apart from that, there is damage to the hull; nothing a few sheets of seribdenum, or aluminium even, won't fix. Damage to some of the electronics and the recycler is just about finished."

"Luxmi, you take the electronics and recycler and oversee the repairs. Hani. You need to source a new motor. There are certainly a couple of spares for the POD in stores, and who knows what else. See what you can dig up. It just needs to get to Mars. Sorry Captain but this need only be a one-way ticket."

"Fine with me," he replied.

I made a quick trip to the POD and sent a short encoded data burst to Duffy:

> All forces on Earth to move in 51 hours: 1 am
> EST, Wednesday is zero hour.

It would take that long to get a message through to Los Angeles and Washington, probably longer, but we had no more time.

***

Zero Hour -50

I caught up with Osei in the bar. He hugged a can of beer in those huge paws while I had only a cup of lime-water.

"The JFK is gone!" Somebody remarked.

Mention of the John F. Kennedy, a huge ore-carrier converted into a space Battleship, during those far off days when the Ischians were a distant rumour, brought back fond memories. I had only visited it once, twenty years ago, on a training mission with Stone, who some-how managed to talk his cousin into taking us to the leg-endary Gass Bar. My reputation might have had some-thing to do with our ease of induction into those most se-cret of circles. Run strictly 'off the record' and blind-eyed by the top brass, it offered the novelty of three drinks, in-fused with gasses; Helium, Hydrogen and NO2.

The Helium Cola tasted good and of course the burps could be tuned to very high pitches but I didn't try the Laughing Gas Soda or the Hydrogen Aid. I heard that some enterprising souls had tried the last inside highly-pressurised air-locks, where it had an effect like LSD on the brain. It's highly inflammable property made this prank doubly dangerous.

Yes I would miss the JFK. Nearly half a mile long, it must have made in impressive sight to the Ischians but it had always been poorly armed. The Luk-shia would have made short work of her.

"Not drinking General?" asked Osei.

"Nope. Too much to do tonight. You enjoy yourself, though. May be the last chance you get. How was it on Venus then? Sorry to ask but I just want to know. This may be *my* last chance..."

"What can I say? It was bad. We were lucky to get off. But you know what they say about R-Company."

"What..? What did you say?"

"I said, you know what they say about R-Company."

"You mean the Replicant Company? But you can't be … ."

"Well no, not literally. Nowadays, it's a whole battalion; the 23rd Quick Response. Both our surviving battalions are from the 23rd."

"You mean you're all replicants?"

"Yes *sir*! And proud of it. You did a lot to make it that way, *sir*!"

"Thanks!" I answered. I kept talking on autopilot, in shock: apart from Captain Dragodes' crew, probably partly comprised of replicants, I seemed to be the only full-human on board. Looking around me, I suddenly felt very alone. "Catch you later Major. Nice talking to you again."

I left and made for my new quarters, near the bar. I wanted to think. Laying on my bunk, I threw my arm over my face.

Stone thought that I had given up my attempts to write pulp fiction. In fact, I had published three novels about my Chandler-esque gumshoe, Dusty, under the pseudonym Angel T. Dust – well, *I* thought the name quite funny. Only a few copies had sold. Anyway, I thought the idea of a human couple having sex to distract an alien would have fascinated the phlegmatic Dusty although it would have confused him too. If it had been *him* having the sex, after being seduced – Dusty had *always* been seduced – with a raised eyebrow, he would have mumbled;

"Seems like the vixen and her fox are toast."

"It can't be that bad," replied a voice beside me.

"Luxmi!"

She entered silently and stopped at the edge of the bunk.

"I'm tired," she replied. "We got the work started on Dragodes' ship. I put some grunts on it now I have kicked it off. Tired of all the attention in the bar, too. I don't know if you noticed but there were a lot of sly comments about you like; 'Glad it isn't me!' That sort of thing. A lot of people assume we are together and asked me who the female volunteer will be."

"Oh. Yes, I did notice a kind of … atmosphere. There were a few sidelong glances. Believe me, *I* wish it wasn't *me*!"

"Can I stay with you, tonight? They … ." Her comment trailed off but I knew what she wanted to say.

"Of course." She curled up beside me in her customary foetal position. I stroked the hair on her head and said:

"It's growing back."

"Liar. So who *is* going to be the other volunteer?" she asked, speaking into my armpit. "Assuming you want to prolong the charade as long as possible, and therefore need an *attractive* female of the species."

Her logic struck me as ice cold and accurate.

"I was going to ask for a volunteer from the two new battalions..."

As if it were some kind of answer, she rose up and kissed me softly on my cheek, my chin and then my mouth. We made love again. This time it felt much more relaxed. After we finished, Luxmi seemed a bit distant from me. I held on to her and asked:

"What's wrong?"

"Jake. You thought you were a replicant once … I *am* a replicant. You know what it feels like. I want to know, what are the main differences between being a replicant and a full-human?"

I smiled but a moment later, she added:

"Only you can tell me."

"You really want to know the truth baby?"

She nodded.

"There's *no* difference, as far as *we* are concerned. I still have exactly the same doubts now that I had then. Faith is hard for anyone to find… and harder to keep. It seems to be particularly difficult for Ischians so you are not in the worst situation."

She smiled. "Thanks." She gave me a little kiss.

"But!" I added. "There is still a difference, and its one created by society … ."

"What?"

"Class. There is still a class distinction."

"Yeah… I know…"

We both put on our headbands to keep up to date with events in the Control Room and on the Station. Seeing a time of 3 am, I checked with the guard posts. There had been no Ischian activity, yet.

"I want to volunteer," Luxmi said, almost whispering. I felt my pulse quicken. I felt angry.

I checked with Hani but there had been no alternative plans submitted before the deadline. He had already begun planning the mission. I kissed Luxmi once on the forehead.

After a long pause, during which time my mind played out a number of scenarios, I finally said, "Makes sense." She stroked the hairs on my forearm. "I thought about stopping you but, actually, your technical knowledge will be hard to beat. And you're a woman. And attractive."

She elbowed me in the ribs. "I want to do it because I don't want you to die; you need looking after. And if I pose as a civilian, it will give you another advantage. We better get up and start planning then."

"Yep! Are you gonna help me get everything together for the meeting?"

"Of course," she replied, pulling on her combat trousers. "You coming?"

"I need some time on my own. I need to talk to my Ischian friend and … wait! Can you do something for me? I showed you the link to Muna on the laser transceiver. Can you set up a vidlink for 10 am with Muna, Duffy and … DeTunne? Tell them they have to get him sober and communicative. I don't care what it takes. There is so much to organise!"

"Okay. See you later," she said, pulling on her T-shirt last and closing the door.

It proved extremely hard to focus my mind on the Paths of the Universal-mind but finally I managed to contact Kek.

"Master," I began, addressing him with due respect. "How do things proceed with your voyage?"

"In less than two months, I will reach Vîentxa."

"And you really think you will find signs of your God, Vîu, there,"

"Yes, I believe so. How are you, Jake?"

"We are very close to launching our... counter-attack. I don't have much time. I need you to ask Ambi-xjhu for more information about the Lukshia, basic stuff like: what sort of internal security system do they use; what deck is the Commander's cabin on, and the cabin number if possible; what deck is the main drive on; what deck are the main recycling units on and how do we disable the drive. That sort of thing. Anything you can tell us would be useful. Please try and get back to me within four Earth hours. Contact me with all the strength you have. I will immediately come to my room and talk with you."

I stopped talking but Kek seemed slow to respond:

"If Ambi-xjhu is busy or distracted, he might ignore me Jake. I will do my best."

"Thanks. I have to go. Oh, tell Ambi-xjhu to be ready to launch his own attack. I don't know when ours will be, yet, but it will be soon. Now he is leader of the Rebels, he should have enough time to plan something."

I faced the biggest challenge of any commander in Earth's history, and with very little time to get anything organised. My mind had become a tumult of ideas and doubts. I lay on my bunk, thinking deeply for half an hour. Then I left quickly to find Luxmi.

"Cancel the work on the freighter," I told her. "I have a better use for it. Did you set up the meeting with Muna?"

"Yes."

"Great. You and I are going to Earth. Come with me. We have a lot of planning to do."

***

Zero Hour -38

Kek-suîxjh contacted me, only thirty minutes late, and gave me the information I required, and more. I had my video conference with Muna's camp so when the last briefing arrived at noon, I felt we were beginning to form a workable plan. All three cruisers had been refuelled and were almost ready to go; they only needed their air pumped back. The freighter still needed an engine. But that suited my plan.

We crammed in every officer down to the rank of Sergeant, even though many had to stand in the corridor; I wanted to address them all.

"I hope you've all managed to get a fair bit of sleep, despite being drunk," I began, grinning. One of the watch officers appeared in the doorway and gestured for my attention. "Just a moment." I beckoned him to me and he whispered in my ear. I turned back to my audience. "Well, they're here. According to the Station's radar, the enemy are massing a few thousand miles from here; perhaps fifty light cruisers. We knew it was going to happen. I want us all, apart from a few, off this Station within two hours. Here's what we're gonna to do. All of you listen very carefully because I don't have time to repeat myself."

"Colonel Mayer, yours is the most difficult, and critical task. You're going to cram as many men as you can get into one of the cruisers and evade capture until you get the signal from Muna's camp on Earth. She will give you a time, probably as little as two hours away, when you must approach the Lukshia. Luxmi will fill you all of you in on the transmission frequencies and codes. Now this could be as long as 36 hours so you will need two sets of breathing gear for most of your men; one set to keep them alive on board; one for another task I will detail in a moment. When you approach the Lukshia, your men on the flight deck should be dressed in Ischian suits. Pick your tallest men. And it may be an idea to repaint the codes on the nose of your cruiser so take some paint. Language guides can be downloaded on all your headbands. Now, if Luxmi and I succeed in our part of the mission, you will be able to signal that you are coming aboard for resupply, and you will be admitted. From the Hangar Deck, Deck 70B, your men should disperse and take control of two vital areas; Deck 53B, the main drive, and Deck 41, the main recycling tanks and pumps. If you deploy fast enough, you shouldn't meet much resistance at first. Most of the combat troops will be on the lowest decks and I have timed this to be during their down-time. If all this goes well, Luxmi and I will find you on Deck 70B as soon as we can. If it goes *badly*, hold that hangar. With the Hangar Deck we can admit other cruisers and possibly escape. That is your strong-hold. Questions?"

"What sort of security system do they have?"

"Retina-recognition. You will need captives... or eyes of captives."

"Two more. What if you don't arrive?"

"Then, you're in command. You will take over leadership of the operation as best you can. My advice would be to blow the ship if all else fails. At least this will break the field around Earth and give others a chance to break out."

"Right you are! We won't let you down! Now, last question… I hear from Major Davidos that we have an Ischian in cold storage… Why can't we use him, her, it … to bluff our way in? We could also use it for the Retina-recognition … ."

"No good. That Ischian is too sick. Deep shoulder wound. She's lost a lot of blood. We tried to care for her I think it's too late. I don't think she will last a day."

"Damn!"

"Major Osei to Mars," I continued.

"Cool!"

"You will take one of the other cruisers and 200 men. Hopefully the ship's recycler can cope with that, since the aliens are twice our size. I cannot advise you on exactly what to do when you get there. The basic idea will be to free the four battalions that are trapped there, and supply them with the transport to fight for us. On the way there, you're going to have to fight. Expect Mars to be heavily defended. I'm confident you will get through. Choose your men but please leave behind any experienced with missile systems. I'll explain why in a moment. Any questions?"

"One. Can I have more men?"

"No. The Lukshia's critical to any kind of fight back. I need all the men I can get for that. Hani, you, Luxmi and I will be going to Earth first, in the third cruiser. We'll be taking the remaining men but no more than fifty. I don't want to deplete our forces by more than that. As I understand it, a fast cruiser might just break through the field that will be around Earth now... if we hit it on the equator. For my plan to work, Luxmi and I must seem to be desperate down-and-outs. That means we need to be on Earth. We will drop you at Muna's camp where we will pick up a friend of mine, DeTunne, and continue on to a Rebel camp just outside Washington. From there, De-Tunne will go into the dome and organise the blanker session. I have already put out feelers... Hani, I already spoke to Muna. You will take a small group of Rebels, including one from Washington, a girl called Tam, and head for Los Angeles as fast as you can. Tam will help you get inside the dome where you can help coordinate the uprising. It will be led by one Adam Enquine."

I expected the ensuing boos and hisses. Adam and his father, Gary were the first to be 'turned' by the Ischians using special psycho-controlling neck-bands. Now they needed to redeem themselves. I held up my hands to quell the audience reaction.

"Gary was, is, a friend of mine. It wasn't their fault, what happened. The Rebels trust them, and so should we. If all goes well, Hani, your group will join up with Muna's and Washington's group. You can rely on Muna for support. She has a vast network of contacts so make the most of it. I suggest that Muna be made the focal-point for the rebellion on Earth: she is tough, resourceful and charismatic. Any questions?"

"What do we do for weapons sir?"

"Muna will have weapons. I am promoting you to Major, Hani."

"Captain Dragodes, am I right in thinking that, occasionally, Rebel traders have boarded Ischian ships? For trade, I mean?"

"Well, not usually this side of the worm-hole … . I am not speaking for myself, but it does happen, yes."

"Right. You will take your stricken freighter, and attempt to board the Lukshia, under the pretence of seeking aid. The damage to your ship is the ideal pretext. You will also tell them your cargo is alcohol. I have heard they love their drink. But Ischians are not as resistant to its effects as us. You and your men will pack as many crates of the remaining beer into your ship as you can. But the beer will be spiked with 95% ethanol: there is a store of it on board and plenty of barrels to mix it in. You will also take fifty of Osei's men and hide them on board. I am sure you can find somewhere; under the floor panels for instance. Wherever you normally hide contraband."

Laughter greeted my little joke. Drogodes looks indignant at first but then grinned, showing a poor set of teeth.

"Every good campaign needs a backup and you're it Captain Drogodes. You will go in, one hour ahead of Colonel Mayer but do nothing until after zero hour. If all is going well, your men can act as Colonel Mayer's reserve and, if not, then do what you can to incapacitate the Ischian crew with alcohol and then take Deck 53B or Deck 41. If you can't get on board, hang around for a while. If all else fails, come back here to refit or head for Mars. Understood?"

"Yes General."

"One more thing … . As of now, you're a Major in the USAC."

"Lastly, there is the question of this Station, J5. We need it. I want it to survive. If all else fails on Earth, it can offer a refuge; sanctuary. Therefore I want the best missile men to stay behind. Ten will do. Colonel, you should assign some of yours, too. There is an on-board missile defence system, but it's not functioning. Get it working and defend the Station. Major Osei, put somebody in charge, will you? I think that's all folks. Any more questions?"

"Not a question, but a suggestion," piped up Sergeant Baker from the doorway. "If you take the battleship, why not call it the Lucky She?"

"Ha! It's a good idea. I hadn't thought of that. We will. Now gentlemen, and gentlewomen, it's time to go. Good luck to you all! You know what to do. And you know what you've *got* to do. Everyone is to be off this station, apart from the missile crew, before 2 pm."

I took a deep breath and stepped into the crowd heading for the door. I burned now with an anger that would not be put out. I could only give in to this emotion because, at last, I sensed a small shift in the mood among my soldiers.

Luxmi came up to me.

"You make a fine speech, General!" she said.

✳✳✳

Biography of Lazlo Ferran

Lazlo Ferran: Exploring the Landscapes of Truth.

Educated near Oxford, during English author Lazlo Ferran's extraordinary life, he has been an aeronautical engineering student, dispatch rider, graphic designer, full-time busker, guitarist and singer, recording two albums. Having grown up in rural Buckinghamshire Lazlo says:

"The beautiful Chiltern Hills offered the ideal playground for a child's mind, in contrast to the ultra-strict education system of Bucks."

Brought up as a Buddhist, he has travelled widely, surviving a student uprising in Athens and living for a while in Cairo, just after Sadat's assassination. Later, he spent some time in Central Asia and was only a few blocks away from gunfire during an attempt to storm the government buildings of Bishkek in 2006. He has a keen interest in theologies and philosophies of the Far East, Middle East, Asia and Eastern Europe.

After a long and successful career within the science industry, Lazlo Ferran left to concentrate on writing, to continue exploring the landscapes of truth.

From the author:

Thank you for reading my story and I hope you liked it. I value very much feedback from people and need this if each book is to be better than the last, so if you could take the time to either post a comment on my amazon page or my blog or simply email me, I would appreciate it.

Where to find Lazlo Ferran
Blog: http://www.lazloferran.com

Amazon: www.amazon.com/author/lazlo_ferran
Email: lazloferran@gmail.com

www.ingramcontent.com/pod-product-compliance
Lightning Source LLC
Chambersburg PA
CBHW070501120726
47910CB00003B/1088